Mysteries of the Macabre
A Halloween Anthology

by

Alexa Day, Alicia Dean
Renci Denham, Elvy Howard
Rohn Federbush
and Leah St. James

This is a work of fiction. Names, characters, places, and incidents either are the product of the authors' imagination or are used fictitiously, and any resemblance to actual persons living or dead, business establishments, events, or locales, is entirely coincidental.

"Scarred" by Alicia Dean – COPYRIGHT © 2015

"Grandma's Way" by Elvy Howard – COPYRIGHT © 2015

"Blood Moon" by Leah St. James – COPYRIGHT © 2015

"Three, After Midnight" by Alexa Day – COPYRIGHT © 2015

"The Timeshare Trip" by Renci Denham – COPYRIGHT © 2015

"The Farm Stray" by Rohn Federbush – COPYRIGHT © 2015

All rights reserved. No part of this book may be used or reproduced in any manner whatsoever without written permission of the author or Edward Allen Publishing, LLC, except in the case of brief quotations embodied in critical articles or reviews.

Digital ISBN 978-0-9853123-8-1
Print ISBN 978-0-9967663-0-2

For information about our authors and/or their availability for live or online events, contact our marketing manager at dprice@edwardallenpublishing.com

Cover and Book Design by David Price

Manufactured in the United States of America
10 9 8 7 6 5 4 3 2 1

Edward Allen Publishing, LLC

PO Box 7769

Hampton, Virginia 23666

www.EdwardAllenPublishing.com

TABLE OF CONTENTS

SCARRED by Alicia Dean

Paranormal Romance

Is Natalie's ability to uncover secrets with a simple touch a blessing or a curse?

GRANDMA'S WAY by Elvy Howard

General Fiction

Will unearthed secrets lead to Caroline's salvation or downfall?

BLOOD MOON by Leah St. James

Paranormal Suspense

It's Halloween, and Ronnie can't shake the feeling that the Harvest Moon Slasher has returned.

THREE, AFTER MIDNIGHT by Alexa Day

Erotic Paranormal Romance (explicit sexuality)

Neither time, nor death, can break the bonds of passion between Deidre and her husband, Cameron.

THE TIMESHARE TRIP by Renci Denham

Satirical Fiction

How many of the Seven Deadly Sins can Crystal and Roy commit in one seven-day cruise?

THE FARM STRAY by Rohn Federbush

General Fiction

The discovery of an abandoned farm in the Michigan countryside triggers a vision of the farmer's past—or is it more?

Scarred

by

Alicia Dean

Chapter One

Simon Cordell left his dark, empty home and headed deep into the woods. As usual, he was restless, filled with too many memories and no longer able to stand his own company. The nighttime suited him. The darkness and density of the woods helped hide his disfigured face…his guilty soul.

Light from a full moon sifted through spidery branches of the wintry trees. From the distance, the howl of a wolf filtered to him—eerie…haunting.

Frigid wind bit through his coat, but he welcomed the pain. Pain made him aware he was still human, that his tragic act from one year ago today hadn't rendered him the unfeeling monster he sometimes felt himself to be.

The soft ground gave beneath his feet. Tree limbs

whipped against him as he plodded through the thickets. The sting of the branches, the piercing icy wind on his exposed flesh, were all welcome sensations. He was alive, although he had no right to be.

The sound of music and cheerful voices interrupted his self-recrimination. He peered between the trees where a faint light shone. As if he had no control of his own body, his feet took him toward the light…toward the sound. From the edge of the woods, he stood, staring at the mayor's mansion. Guests in colorful finery exited vehicles and made their way up the path to the door.

Simon was about to step back, to fade into obscurity, when a particular guest caught his attention. His heartbeat sped up. He nearly called out her name but stopped himself just in time. Dark hair framed her pale face. Beneath her black cloak, the skirt of an emerald green gown floated around her. The woman paused for a moment and glanced in his direction. He slunk back behind a tree, pulse pounding. Had she seen him? He didn't know. He did know that he had to see *her*. Had to get a closer look at the woman he hadn't seen in ten years but had been unable to erase from his memory.

****

Natalie Jayne caught her breath and whirled toward

the copse of trees at the edge of the property. Some… force compelled her to turn, though she hadn't actually seen or heard anything. Her gaze sought out the source of the odd feeling. She squinted against the snow that drifted down and nearly obscured her vision. Nothing. She shook her head. Just an overactive imagination.

Taking a deep breath, she turned away from the woods and back to the mansion. Kristopher's mansion. She gave a wistful smile. Hard to believe the boy she'd known, had grown up with, was now mayor of Westbury.

She cast one last glance over her shoulder to the woods. A shudder ran through her she couldn't explain. Ignoring it, she tramped through the snow to the door. One thing she didn't miss about Maine was the weather. A blizzard on Halloween. Living in Oklahoma for the past ten years had almost made her forget how harsh Maine winters could be, and how early they could descend.

A gray-haired butler took her cloak at the door. The ballroom was filled to near capacity. Most of the attendees wore costumes. Just off the dance floor was a stage where a twenty-four by thirty-six photo of Jessica stood on an easel with candles arrayed around it. Today was not only her birthday, it was the anniversary of her tragic death. The lovely girl Natalie knew had developed into a beautiful woman. Silver-blonde hair and a flawless face, sky-blue eyes framed by dark lashes. She was smiling in the photo, unaware death would take her much too soon.

Natalie pushed aside the morose thought and the rush of guilt over missing her funeral. She'd been in Paris on business and hadn't had a choice, but she was here now. Hopefully, Jessica knew that. Knew she cared, even though they hadn't seen one another since they were eighteen. She should have been back to visit. But she'd been a coward. She hadn't been able to bear the thought of returning when Jessica and Simon began dating. How could she watch the two of them together, wishing it could be her?

And now, Jessica was dead, and she'd never have the opportunity to see her one last time. The circumstances surrounding her death had been suspicious, but Natalie would never believe Simon had killed her on purpose. It had been a terrible accident. And he'd almost died himself. The Simon she'd known had been reckless, wild, but not a killer.

****

An hour later, after returning home to change clothes, Simon arrived at the mayor's opulent manor, wearing a black tux and pale blue shirt. His strategically formed black mask hid the top three quarters of his face, showing only his mouth and chin. Fortunately, the event was a costume party. He'd be damned if he would show himself—his true self—in public. Which begged the question, what the hell was he doing here? He had called himself all kinds of a fool for coming tonight, but no matter how much he'd argued, his heart had won, and here he was.

When the door opened, Simon gave the butler a curt nod, then strode through the foyer into the ballroom. He scanned the crowd. Servers in white uniforms with black bowties moved amongst the guests, holding trays of champagne. Almost like a celebration. But that wasn't the case. Everyone in the room, most especially the mayor, was grieving for Jessica Thacker. She was well loved in Westbury, where she'd grown up. Where the four of them had grown up together, Simon, Jessica, Natalie, and the mayor. How things had changed since that time—drastically, tragically. The mayor wouldn't welcome Simon to the party. He would have him forcibly removed if he saw him. But Simon didn't plan to be here long enough for that to happen. He would only stay a few moments, just long enough to see Natalie.

Weaving through the crowd, he ignored the curious glances cast his way. He had only one focus. He rounded the room twice, but Natalie was nowhere to be seen.

He stalked toward the balcony, badly in need of fresh air. He had been a recluse this past year and being around so many people stole his ability to breathe. He eagerly swept open the balcony doors and stepped out—and saw her. Her profile faced him. The full moon wrapped her in its glow, her features clearly defined. Smooth, pale skin and full, red lips.

He must have made a sound, because she turned an alarmed gaze on him.

Her gloved hand flew to her chest, and she gave a self-conscious laugh. "Oh my, you startled me."

She was stunning in a Marie Antoinette costume and had fortunately foregone a wig. Her ebony hair was swept back from her face with a few stray tendrils caressing her cheeks. Her beauty stole his breath as effectively as the crowd had, and it took a few moments before he could speak. "I'm sorry. I didn't mean to frighten you."

"You didn't frighten me. I just thought I was alone." She gestured to the opaque glass door that separated them from the partygoers. "I was feeling claustrophobic, so I came out here."

He smiled. "So you chose frostbite over claustrophobia?"

She laughed again—a dazzling sound that had his

knees threatening to buckle. Her blue eyes sparkled, and her features lit with delight. She was a sight to behold. For one brief, insane moment, he wished he could spend the rest of his life making her laugh, putting that glow on her face.

She'd matured nicely from the awkward but lovely teen he'd known. Without the cloak, every perfect curve was revealed. She wrapped her arms around herself, her teeth chattering in the frigid air.

Simon took off his coat and stepped toward her. The scent of vanilla and spice rose to his nostrils, sending heat rushing through his blood. He pushed back an urge to step closer, to sweep her up in his arms, taste those delectable lips. Instead, he draped the coat over her shoulders. "Here. Take this so you don't freeze to death."

"Thank you." She accepted the coat, then glanced to the doors. "I suppose I should go back inside."

He bit his tongue to keep from begging her to stay.

****

In spite of her intent to go inside, Natalie remained rooted in place. There was something intriguing about this man, something that made her want to know more about him. Not badly enough to remove her gloves and use her gift, however. She'd sworn off doing that, other than for emergencies. But she had to admit she was tempted to get the answers to the questions spinning through her mind. Who was he? What did he look like beneath the mask? What would it feel like to touch him…?

She shook her head. What an insanely inappropriate direction her mind had taken. She couldn't allow herself the luxury of touching others. Not if she wanted to keep her secret…and not if she wanted to keep from learning the secrets of others. Besides, this man was a stranger…a *masked* stranger. She should be afraid…or at least wary. But she was neither.

She shivered and drew the cloak more tightly around her shoulders. "I'm Natalie."

He hesitated a few moments, then said, "Pleased to meet you. I'm Jonathan."

"Nice to meet you too." She almost asked him about the mask, but instead said, "Are you from here? Did you know Jessica?"

"I live nearby. I knew her, yes. You?"

"I knew her a long time ago." Sadness made her heart heavy. She should have stayed in touch. "I used to live here, but I moved away. I haven't been back in several years."

"What made you stay away?" His voice dropped, and he seemed to be listening intently, as if her reply mattered.

"I—I was busy. I'm a fashion buyer and I travel often. And…" She drew in a deep breath. "Well, you know…"

"No, I don't know." He narrowed his eyes. "I sense there's more."

She smiled. "You're very intuitive." She didn't tell him that she'd left because she was tired of being the oddity in town. She wasn't blind to the covert looks, the whispers and jeers, the way many of the townspeople avoided eye contact. As her affliction developed and grew more powerful, it became more difficult to hide. Especially after the incident her sophomore year of high school. She was being honored with Student of the Year, and when she accepted the award from their beloved principal, their hands touched. Images like a slide show flashed through her mind. Mr. Benson had been secretly taking photos of female students in the gym showers. An investigation uncovered inappropriate pictures on his home computer, and he'd ultimately been convicted and sentenced to prison. Although everyone agreed what he'd done was heinous and needed to be discovered, blame rested heavily on Natalie. If she weren't such an aberration, they might have never known, and could have continued living in blissful ignorance, their ideal of the adored Mr. Benson still intact.

After that, she'd taken to wearing gloves and avoiding contact with people as much as possible, which only enhanced her loner, freak image. The only people who had stuck by her were Simon, Jessica, and Kristopher. At the time, hers and Simon's relationship had just begun developing into something beyond friendship, but she quickly backed off. The thought of discovering a horrifying secret about him was more than she could bear.

She and her parents moved away after graduation, and with time, she had learned to control her curse. The visions only came when she touched someone with her bare hands, so she wore gloves most of the time. Fortunately, in the clothing industry, she was considered to be making a slightly eccentric fashion statement. She'd even designed her own line of gloves, which were selling quite nicely. No one ever had to discover she'd done it to hide her affliction. She simply made sure contact with others was kept at a minimum, and when necessary, very brief. She'd never had a lover, not wanting to confront the issue of their wondering why she insisted on keeping her gloves on during lovemaking. Bonding with another person on an emotional level was a luxury she couldn't afford. But that was a small price to pay for peace of mind.

With a mental shake, she brought herself back to the present. "I suppose there were just too many painful memories."

"A beautiful woman like you should never feel pain."

She tried to laugh, but it caught in her chest. It was more than the words, it was the intense way he delivered them.

He inclined his head toward the balcony door where music from the ballroom filtered out to them, then held out a hand. "Perhaps a dance will warm you?"

As if her heart tugged her forward, she was powerless to resist. Something unexpected and magical was taking place. She wanted to explore it, to hold onto the sensation as long as she could.

He took her hand and placed his on the small of her back. She moved across the snow-dusted balcony in his arms, lost in the strains of *The Blue Danube*, lost in the dark eyes behind the mask.

He put his lips to her ear. "You feel like heaven and smell like an exotic garden."

His voice was deep, raspy. Goosebumps that had nothing to do with the cold pricked her skin. Her breath stalled in her chest. "Thank you," she managed through a dry throat.

He didn't move away. His face was so close that

if she turned, ever so slightly… Before she could stop herself, her head tilted so that their eyes met and their lips were almost touching. His hold on her tightened, his ebony eyes glittered, and then he dipped his head, and his lips met hers with an explosion of desire that had her clinging to his broad shoulders. His mouth was firm and warm, and she moved closer to him, seeking a deeper connection, wanting more of this crazy beautiful feeling.

"Let me see your face," she whispered against his mouth.

His muscles tensed beneath her hand and he drew back, shaking his head. "No, please don't ask that of me." His raspy tone took on a note of desperation. "Let me have this night. I'm certain there will never be another. I'll never again feel the way I feel now."

She studied the entreaty in his gaze, then nodded and rested her head on his chest, listened to his heartbeat. Seconds ticked by while they remained in their wintery cocoon. She was so consumed by the strange and wonderful joy coursing through her, she barely noticed the balcony door opening.

A voice cut through the silence. "Excuse me." She looked up to find the mayor's aide in the doorway. "The mayor is making a speech, so you might want to come in."

"Of course, thank you." She gave Simon a regretful look. "Perhaps we should."

He jerked a brief nod. "After you."

A small part of her was relieved at the interruption. She needed a break from the strange spell gripping her. What was it about this man that made her feel as if she'd known him a lifetime?

Chapter Two

Simon debated slipping out the door without listening to the speech. There was nothing Kristopher Martensen could say that he wanted to hear. He would no doubt extol Jessica's virtues, paint her in a perfect light. But Simon knew the truth, as did Kristopher. Although he'd loved Jessica, he'd learned her true nature the night of her death.

But he didn't want to leave Natalie, not just yet. They stood side by side, the warmth from her body reaching out to him, keeping him in place as firmly as a steel cable.

Kristopher stood on a small stage at the end of the ballroom. He wore a white tux with a black tie, his blond hair glowing like a halo, although the image was deceiving. The man was as duplicitous as Satan himself.

He spoke into the microphone, his voice booming throughout the cavernous room. "I would like to thank each and every one of you for coming tonight, to not only pay tribute to Jessica Thacker and her death, but to celebrate her life." He grew silent and cleared his throat. When he spoke again, his voice was hoarse. "She was a special person, a beautiful soul who loved people, loved life. She would be honored to see the number of people who gathered to pay homage."

The crowd erupted in cheers. When they quieted, Kristopher said, "While this is a night of reverence and honor, it's also a night to remember the brutal, senseless way that she died. Although the monster responsible is free, we must never forget, never let him live in peace. Simon Cordell is free to live his life, while our beloved Jessica lies in a cold grave."

Simon's heart sped up. Although the people in the room didn't know he was here, he could feel their anger, their accusation. His skin burned with the heat of their ire. He stepped back, planning to retreat, when Natalie spoke.

"That's not fair!" Her voice rose in the momentary silence. "Simon was absolved of her death, and you need to let him be."

Kristopher's gaze swung to her. "Natalie Jayne?"

Even from this distance, Simon could see red suffuse Kristopher's face. "You have no right to show up here a year after her death, after not even attending her funeral, and speak of something you know nothing about."

Natalie lifted her skirts and headed toward the stage. Simon wanted to call her back, to keep her from coming to his defense, but she was already approaching the podium.

She moved gracefully up the steps and to the microphone. Kristopher held up his hands as if to push her away, and Simon tensed. If he laid a hand on her…

But he didn't. She drew her shoulders back and faced him down. He took a step back, and she spoke into the microphone to the crowd. "You should be ashamed of yourselves. Simon loved Jessica. He was going to marry her. The accident nearly killed him as well. How can you stand in judgment of a man who's suffered so greatly?"

"He's a murderer!" someone shouted.

Several voices joined in agreement.

Natalie lifted her voice above the others. "The investigation uncovered no wrongdoing. Isn't it time you let him live in peace?"

The crowd roared its displeasure. A mixture of admiration and protectiveness gripped Simon's chest.

She was so brave, so beautiful. But so misguided. He cringed and headed to the stage.

****

Natalie wasn't sure what had possessed her to make a spectacle of herself. She just couldn't bear to hear these people crucify Simon. Especially since he wasn't here to defend himself.

Kristopher clenched his fists as if he were using all his willpower not to throttle her. "What the hell do you think you're doing, Natalie?" He spoke low enough that the people in the ballroom couldn't hear him. His blue eyes were tortured, his handsome face drawn in pain and grief. "You were her friend. You should want justice."

"Justice is one thing. You people are out for blood. You've known Simon your whole life. He would never have hurt Jessica—or anyone—on purpose."

"You've been gone for ten years. People change."

She captured his gaze, searched for some sign of compassion. "Do you really, deep in your heart, believe he killed her in cold blood?"

"I know he did."

"Why would he do that?"

His mouth twisted with bitterness. "Jealousy. Rage."

"Jealousy over what?"

"Me. Jessica and I. She told him that night that she was leaving him. For me. We were in love and were going to be together."

Sick dread coiled in her stomach. "No, that's not true."

"Oh, but it is. He was controlling, obsessive." Tears filled his eyes, and he shook his head. "I should never have let her tell him on her own."

A niggle of doubt wormed its way into her heart. Simon had been a good man, but he was also capable of strong emotion…strong passion. If the woman he loved betrayed him with another—with his best friend—what might he have done in a moment of mindless rage?

"He's right."

Natalie whirled at the deep voice to find the phantom from the balcony behind her.

"What do you mean, he's right? What do you know of Jessica and Simon?"

His lips tightened, but he remained silent.

"I'll tell you what he knows." Kristopher's words were like the growl of a wounded animal. "He knows everything about that night. He's the one who killed her."

Natalie frowned. "I don't understand…" With narrowed eyes, she stared at the phantom—correction, at Simon. She gasped as betrayal sliced like a knife her upper arms and pulled her to him. "I am a monster, can't you see that?" His jaw tightened and the words shot from him like bullets. "I may not have killed Jessica on purpose, but I wanted her dead."

****

As the lies fell from his lips, Simon's chest felt as though it would cave in under the weight of Natalie's pain. She looked so stricken, so disappointed. He steeled his resolve. Better to disappoint her now than to destroy her later. She had to see.

There was one guaranteed way to show her who he truly was.

Summoning his courage, he gripped the edge of his mask. His hands grew clammy. Could he really give up its protection? The ballroom was filled to capacity. Hundreds of curious eyes stared at him. People would see his repulsive countenance. But he had to make Natalie see. Had to show her his true self. He jerked the mask from his face and flung it to the floor of the stage. A cacophony of gasps swelled around him, but he paid them no mind. His focus was on the woman before him, her eyes rounded in horror. "This is who I am, Natalie. The boy you knew is gone."

Inhaling deeply, Simon stepped from the stage and strode through the ballroom. Ignoring the stares, the gasps, the murmurs, he forged through bodies toward the exit.

He was unable to draw a full breath until he reached the night air. Even then, his breath would barely push through the band around his heart. He closed his eyes against the image of Natalie's shocked expression. At least he had the bittersweet comfort of knowing he'd never see her again.

****

Natalie swallowed back tears. Simon's handsome face…scarred. The laughter and jeers of the crowd penetrated her numbness. Simon said he… Surely he was lying. He wouldn't really want Jessica dead, would he? Regardless, these people were behaving like savages.

She stalked back to the microphone. "I hope you're all pleased with yourselves. You've tortured a man who's already tortured himself more than most humans could bear. He made a mistake. Have you no empathy, no forgiveness in you?"

"Forgiveness won't bring Jessica back!" someone in the crowd shouted. A chorus of agreement rose.

"No, no it won't. Nothing can bring her back. All we can do is move on. Jessica would want us to."

Kristopher pushed to the microphone. "You have no idea what Jessica would want. You left her. She was one of the few people who supported a mutant like you, and this is how you repay her?"

She flinched, and heat burned her cheeks. He was right. Jessica, Kristopher, and Simon had befriended her in spite of her curse. They'd shown her kindness. And now Jessica was dead, Simon was accused of her murder, and Kristopher was heartbroken, devastated.

"I'm sorry," she whispered. "I know you must be grieving, but do you think Jessica would want this for you?" The crowd quieted and seemed to fade into non-existence as she shut off the mic and waited for Kristopher's reply.

He blinked back fresh tears. "Please, just go."

Something in his face alerted her instincts. He was holding back secrets. If she were going to help him, help Simon, she had to know. Slipping off her glove, she took Kristopher's hand.

He looked at their clasped hands, then at her face. His eyes widened. "Oh no. No, you don't." He tried to jerk away, but she held tight.

The visions came, revealing the truth as though she were with them in the last few moments of Jessica's life.

Chapter Three

Images assaulted her…Kristopher and Jessica lying in bed. Kristopher's voice came to her as clearly as though he were speaking now. "I love you. I want us to be together."

Jessica's reply: "I can't leave Simon."

"But you love me."

"I love you both."

The scene faded and the interior of a car—illuminated only by the lights on the instrument panel—took their place. Simon driving. Jessica in the passenger seat. A screen on the dash lighting with a video. Jessica's hand going to her mouth as the scene played out. She and Kristopher, making love.

Simon's face twisting in pain, disbelief.

Jessica's strangled cry.

An argument ensued. Jessica reached for Simon, took hold of his arm, the wheel jerked, the car careened out of control…

With a cry, Natalie wrenched away from Kristopher, and her eyes flew open. Kristopher stared at her, breathing hard, tears streaming down his face.

"Jessica wasn't going to leave him," Natalie said softly.

"She would have. Eventually. But he killed her."

Natalie slowly shook her head. "No. It was an accident. Why was there a video of you two making love?"

Kristopher squeezed his eyes shut. "You're a freak," he whispered.

"Tell me." In spite of her anger, a glimmer of sympathy rose. He obviously loved Jessica a great deal. People did horrible things in the name of love. She gently touched his arm. "Isn't it time to let go of the anger and grief? Unburden your soul?"

Kristopher covered his face and fell to his knees, sobbing into his hands. "Oh my God, it was my fault. Jessica wouldn't leave him, so I took matters into my own hands."

He halted, great, racking sobs shaking his shoulders. She waited. The crowd had gone silent, as if they waited, too.

He lifted his head and turned a ravaged expression up to her. "They were on their way to the wedding rehearsal dinner, and I couldn't bear it anymore. I sent Simon a video I'd taken of the two of us."

Her heart plummeted into her stomach. She nearly went to her knees with the weight of her sorrow. "All his suffering, all these months. You caused it. All because of your own guilt."

He didn't answer. He bent his head back down and continued weeping.

"He never told anyone? About the video? About the role you played?"

Kristopher shook his head, his hands still covering his face.

"Maybe you're the monster." The words were cruel, but Kristopher had wronged Simon greatly. Had used the town he loved against him, all for his own gain.

Kristopher dropped his hands and lifted his tear-stained face. "I am. You're right."

"You need to make things right." She gestured toward the crowd. "With them."

Kristopher's shoulders slumped, but he stood and moved to the microphone. He hesitated, his features seeming to have aged ten years. He turned on the mic and slowly started to speak. "Please, may I have your attention? I have something to say." He shot a look at Natalie. "Something I should have said a year ago."

Natalie nodded and stepped back. Without warning, a jolt pinged her chest. A delicious ache, an undeniable, uncontrollable compulsion to find Simon enveloped her.

She rushed off the stage, through the crowd to the front door and jerked it open. Party lights illuminated the large yard. She peered through the falling snow. No sign of Simon. She lifted her skirts and flew down the steps.

Mindless of the deepening snow, she raced across the yard as quickly as she could. "Simon!" Her throat ached with tears. He was nowhere in sight. "Simon. Where are you? Can you hear me?"

He lived nearby, just on the other side of the woods. Getting to her car and cleaning off snow would take too much time. The cover of trees would help protect her from the cold, and the snow wasn't as deep there as it was in the open. An urgent, burning desire to reach Simon spurred her on. Please, God, don't let him have done something to harm himself...

No, he wouldn't do that. He was stronger than that. Still, she dove into the woods.

She'd only gone a short distance when she spotted a figure moving ahead of her through the trees. She picked up her pace and reached him, latching onto his arm. "Simon!"

He stopped but didn't face her. "You shouldn't be out here."

"I know what happened," she panted, struggling to regulate her breathing.

He inclined his head. "Then you know how evil I am. Release my arm and leave me be. You'll never have to see me again."

"Look at me, Simon."

He whirled to face her, and she gasped as the depth of his pain seared her.

Sympathy and…love…washed through her. His suffering tugged at her soul. "I know the *truth* about Jessica's death. You weren't to blame."

His jaw clenched. "That doesn't exactly erase it, though, does it?"

Her gaze roamed his face. Jagged white scars ran from the corner of his right eye, down his jawbone. Puckered pink scars marred the flesh on his forehead. The left side of his face was oddly untouched… perfectly handsome.

She released him and lifted her chin. "Your face is not nearly as scarred as your soul. You need to forgive yourself. To find happiness…love."

"Is that so?" A bitter laugh burst from him. He took hold of her shoulders and yanked her close to him, close to his damaged face. His dark eyes were tormented. "What if I told you that I love *you*? That the only way I can find happiness is in your arms? Preposterous, right? Someone as hideous as I with a beauty like you? So do me, and yourself, a favor. Just let me be." He shoved her away and turned, but she grabbed his arm and tugged him back, making him look at her.

"You're beautiful," she whispered. "I love you, too. I have since we were children. When I moved away, and you started seeing Jessica…" She wasn't sure which was worse, the remembered pain or the guilt over her jealousy of a dead woman. "Do you still love her?"

His lips twisted. "I'm not sure I ever did. Not like I should have. When you left, I thought I'd die. My heart shattered. It was all I could do to get through each day." He drew in a deep breath. "Jessica was there for me. Loving, supportive. She made me feel like living again, and I cared for her…but not like I did you." His voice dropped. "Never like I did you."

Natalie's heart soared with joy. "I still love you, Simon. I realized after seeing you again that I never stopped."

He frowned at her for a moment, his disbelief apparent. "How could someone like you ever love someone like me? How could you be happy with me?"

"How could I not?" She lifted a hand to lay it

against his jaw.

He flinched and pulled away. "Please…don't."

Was it his external or internal scars he didn't want her to see? No matter. She would make him see that she loved him…all of him.

"Let me touch you," she whispered. "You don't frighten me. Nothing about you frightens me."

He narrowed his eyes and shook his head. "You can't…you don't want to see…"

She stood on tiptoe and placed a gentle kiss on his jaw. "I do want to see," she murmured against his warm skin. "I'm all in."

When he didn't protest, she pulled back and slid her fingers over the scarred side of his face. He tightened his lips but didn't jerk away. She braced herself for images—for whatever might come, whatever she might learn about Simon. She was ready.

They stood in the chilled silence, waiting. After several seconds, it became clear to her…nothing was happening. No visions, no images. All she felt was a rush of abiding, unconditional love. A sense of rightness.

"What do you see?" His voice was hoarse, his eyes wary.

Letting out a sigh, she smiled. "I see a long, happy future filled with love."

A small grin lifted the corners of his mouth. "Your gift revealed that to you?"

She shook her head. "My heart did. I love you, you love me, that's all I need to know." She would deal with whatever issues her abilities caused in having a real, physical relationship with a man. Nothing could be worse than losing Simon a second time.

His jaw tightened. For a moment, she thought he would refuse, that he would turn away and leave her. Then, with a groan, he slipped his arms around her and pulled her against his chest, fused his lips to hers.

His kiss weakened her knees. For the first time in her life, she cherished the gift she'd always viewed as a curse. It had given her Simon.

Grandma's Way

by

Elvy Howard

Dedication

Dedicated to my 15-year-old granddaughter who is sweet and wonderful and nothing like my protagonist.

"Caroline? Caroline, can you hear me?" Momma sounded pissed. Caroline Turner stuck her head out the attic window. "What?"

On the sidewalk outside the chain-link fence, her face angled up, Caroline's momma yelled up the three stories, "I'm going to get lunch."

"Are you going home, or out somewhere?" Caroline yelled back.

"Home, and you better make a dent up there before I get back, young lady, you hear me?"

Caroline had, and was sure everyone in the neighborhood had, too. "Yeah, yeah." She turned away from the window and back to her own personal nightmare.

Careful not to stir up any of the dust coating an

unimaginable number of things in the stuffy, hot room, she pulled her dark hair into a knot and bent over the long shelves built low and running the length of the eaves. *Young lady, my ass*. At fifteen she didn't feel like a young lady at all.

Mostly she felt her childhood long gone, and adolescence not anything TV had led her to expect.

Squatting to look at an old cardboard shoe box, Caroline lifted the lid. Postcards were crammed so tight, she had to grab some from the center and pry them out to see one. The top postcard, a faded cartoon of a curvy woman in a skimpy bikini with VIRGINIA BEACH! plastered in red letters arching over, greeted her.

On the back was a note from someone named Ben, which only read, *Hope to see you again soon. What a wonderful weekend.*

"Boring." Sitting on the splintery wooden floor, Caroline was glad she'd been made to wear jeans, even if she *was* already sweating. Flipping through the postcards, she noticed they'd been put in order beginning in May of 1962, until the last one in 1987. Her grandmother's last name changed three times in the course of those years—Imogene Walker, Imogene Peterson, and Imogene Jenkins. Walker was her mother's maiden name so he'd been Grandma's first

Grandma's Way

husband.

Grandma's last husband, Grandpa Porter, wasn't represented. She didn't know when Grandma married him. He was only a vague memory, as he died before she was five. Caroline's recollection of him was a big fat man, forever in a bad mood, smoking his fat, smelly cigars on the back porch even when it was cold, because Grandma wouldn't let him smoke inside. Mostly, she remembered avoiding grumpy Grandpa Porter as much as she could.

Flipping through the postcards, she didn't see anyone she recognized. Maybe some were from some far-off relative, but she was pretty sure Momma didn't want them. The shoe box went into a large, black plastic bag. Scooting back, she spied a cigar box, opened it and found some ancient fountain pens, too dried up to ever work again, and some old, unused stamps that only cost three cents.

I wonder who Ben was. Grandma sure had a lot of guys writing her. Maybe she was like some kind of player. Gross, what a strange and weird thing to think about your own grandma. She dismissed thoughts of Grandma's love life from her head.

Thinking the pens and stamps might be worth something, she put them in a large cardboard box Momma had given her.

"We need every dime we can get from this place," Momma had said.

Caroline used to believe that was true. Her entire life she'd bought into the idea they were on the verge of financial collapse. Until right after Grandma died, and Momma got careless about things and left her bank statement on the kitchen counter. Momma had over five grand in her checking account and twenty-three grand in savings.

Caroline still felt the shock of betrayal, her brain like scrambled eggs for days afterwards.

It got Caroline to wondering what else was stored in the locked steel box in Momma's closet.

Momma's cheapness extended into sometimes bizarre levels, like dragging Caroline to funerals of people Momma barely knew, just for the free meal afterwards.

When she was a kid, Caroline didn't mind wearing second-hand clothes, as long as Grandma got her a Christmas dress that wasn't too big. Same for Easter, when some limp rag Momma insisted was just fine, wasn't. *And now I don't even have that.*

Grandma hadn't been the easiest person to be around, but unlike Momma, she'd understood her granddaughter required a few nice things in her life.

Grandma had been a connoisseur of good things,

and until she got sick, had given herself cruises and trips to odd places, like the one to Ireland with a bunch of people to look at old rocks. She'd told Caroline she'd felt the vibrations of the ages in the presence of those rocks. Which was a bunch of hogwash. Grandma was famous for her enthusiasms and fads, but if she'd lived, Grandma would have taken Caroline on the promised cruise when she graduated from high school.

Caroline picked up something that looked like a colorful striped ball of red, yellow, blue and green. It turned out to be rubber bands so old they had melted together. The melted rubber stuck to her hand, even after she grabbed the ball with the inside of the plastic bag and pried it off. Even rubbing them on her jeans didn't get it all off.

Glass ashtrays from everywhere were farther down the shelf. Caroline studied one bearing the logo *Golden Nugget* in angular letters that looked to be from the '50s and scrunched her nose in thought. Could it be valuable? Probably not. The Shop and Save, a consignment store her momma frequented, carried tons of ashtrays. She pitched them in the trash bag.

She stood, sweating and picking up the half-full bag, which was heavier than she thought. Dragging the bag to the front windows, she hoped for a breeze, but there was nothing. A maple tree turning bright red filled the outside of the windows. Some people might think it was pretty, but the red color reflecting into the attic only made the heat feel more intense.

Raising the screen, and leaning outside into air not super-heated in the damn attic, she felt a slight breeze and heard maple leaves rustling. Aiming for the sidewalk, she swung the bag out over the porch. It landed right where she wanted with a righteous smash.

All the glass breaking, the melted rubber-band ball becoming embedded with shards, along with the breeze, became the most delightful thing Caroline had experienced the entire morning.

Until she saw her momma's station wagon pull up. Her momma got out, and not noticing Caroline at all, opened the back of the wagon. Caroline watched her retrieve a bucket filled with cleaning supplies, a brown paper bag, her pocketbook and a small cooler.

Hoping for a cold Pepsi in the cooler, Caroline scanned the room for things to add to the cardboard box. She found some tin boxes covered in grime, but she could make out the advertisements on them for cigarettes and gum. Some dusty tablecloths stacked on top of a bureau followed. The top drawers of the same bureau held faded books, or maybe they were some kind of old-style magazines with soft covers, their childishly colored pictures probably hand-painted, and pages strung with thread. Caroline put them all into the box, which looked respectfully full, and carried it down the back stairs, down the hall to the curved staircase leading to the foyer.

Each downward level became progressively cooler, but it still was a shock to go through the swinging door to air conditioning coming full-blast from the little window at the end of the long kitchen.

Caroline's momma was at the sink. "You only did one bag?" she asked, washing her hands.

"I brought all this down too." Caroline said like a challenge, setting her box onto the red-topped Formica table pushed next to the long left wall, for like, forever.

"Anything good?" Caroline's momma came over and looked inside. "These might be worth something. Lord, your grandma sure squirreled away enough stuff." She took a tin box to the sink, and scrubbed it with a yellow ridged sponge.

Colors came alive under the running water, in shades of teal with gold lettering. Suddenly Caroline wanted that box for herself, for keepsakes or something. "What did you bring for lunch?" she asked, silently deciding to sneak the colorful tin box to a place she knew in the basement, later on, when Momma wasn't looking.

Among all the boxes of plates and glasses wrapped

in newspaper that lined the floor, and the figurines, bowls, kitchen utensils, and measuring cups on the stove and counter, Momma wouldn't miss it.

"In the cooler." Momma nodded at the cooler in a kitchen chair, while she got at the sides of the box with her sponge.

Caroline was disappointed to see bottles of water under peanut butter and jelly sandwiches. Still, the air conditioning felt great and she sat to eat her sandwich.

She drew out the eating process as long as possible while her momma continued to inspect the contents of Caroline's cardboard box. "Where did you find this?" she asked, holding up a book.

"In a dresser, you know, the one in the middle of the attic."

"It looks really old."

"Yeah, I know." Caroline took another bite. "I bet they're worth a bundle."

"I don't know." Momma's eyes were hopeful, turning the pages of black and white pictures with blotched colors of blue, red and green on them. "I think it's some kind of children's book. I might have to get someone to look at these."

"I guess so." Agreeing with Momma sometimes softened her.

"Yeah, maybe go to Milly's Antiques and see who

Grandma's Way

might be able to value this for me."

"That's a really good idea, Momma."

The value of things preoccupied her momma to no end. *Caroline! You shouldn't eat all the cookies—they're for company. Leftovers are just fine for the two of us. Turn off the lights when you leave the room; you know I'm not made of money.*

Hoping the mother-lode of goodies found in the attic might be enough to sway her, Caroline asked, "How about letting me go to the Halloween dance tonight after all?"

"You've got to be kidding me."

"I've been up there sweating all morning, and I found some good stuff."

"All you're doing is what you're supposed to be doing. It's not my fault you're flunking geometry."

"Oh, my God, Momma!"

"Don't be swearing at me, young lady."

Caroline was at a crossroads. She hated Momma so much she wanted to leave the kitchen, slamming the door behind her (which, when she thought about it, wouldn't slam anyway—it being a swinging door and all), or stay in the kitchen, which was at least cool. Cooler than cool actually. The icy air on her sweaty clothes felt deliciously cold.

She reached for another sandwich, even though

she wasn't hungry, and a bottle of barely cold water. "Lord, Momma, you'd think things like Grandma dying weren't supposed to bother me."

"What in the world are you talking about now?"

"I think the reason I can't focus on geometry is because I'm still so sad."

"Get off your soapbox, Caroline. It's not going to work."

Damn, I guess I played out the dead Grandma card. "It's not just that, it's just doing all this stuff is like saying goodbye to her all over again. Getting rid of all her stuff, I mean. Doesn't it bother you at all?"

Slowly chewing the dollar store peanut butter and jelly probably full of chemicals poisoning her, Caroline waited for an answer.

Momma put her rubber gloves back on and began scrubbing another tin box. "It has been a lot of extra work, I know."

"She's barely dead, Momma, and you're just ripping through this place like there's no tomorrow. I mean," Caroline continued, realizing it was true, "we won't even be able to come back and visit, or anything."

"You listen here, young lady, I'm only doing what I have to. It's not like I have anyone to depend on . . ."

Caroline didn't have to listen. She knew exactly

what Momma would go on and on about. But it bothered her, how easy it was for Momma to wipe out any trace of Grandma's life.

It bothered Caroline even more not being able to go to that dance. For the past six weeks, when Bobby Ray was alone after fourth period, Caroline had been working on getting him to notice her.

When beautiful Bobby Ray was leaving Spanish class, Caroline would be going to art, after stopping off at the girls' bathroom to check her lipstick and mascara.

They had progressed from eye contact to nods, and now he was smiling, sometimes stopping for a minute to chat. But he had waited until yesterday to ask if she was coming to the Halloween dance. She'd said yes, smiling into his blue eyes in a way she hoped would encourage him without making her look too easy. Not worrying then about the report card being sent home in the mail that day.

All that work down the drain. Bobby Ray would probably hook up with one of the many girls who wanted to date him, and Momma would probably have her digging through Grandma's shit until after ten.

Momma had stopped talking and was still washing things in the sink.

"Did it ever occur to you that maybe this place is the only real home I ever knew, and maybe it might be hard to say goodbye?"

"We moved away when you were six."

"And back again when I was eight," Caroline shot back, baiting Momma to open up *that* can of worms.

But Momma kept facing the sink and washing and stacking lids, measuring cups, and tin boxes in the dish drainer.

Taking an unwanted bite of stale white bread filled with poison, Caroline chewed on different angles to approach her problem. She'd been chewing on it all morning, because sometimes, when she was smart enough, she could negotiate with the insanity that was her mother. "When are you planning to have all this done?"

"Done?" Momma sat down, leaned over to the cooler and got a sandwich and some water from it.

"All this stuff cleaned out, sold, whatever, sweep the floors, done."

"Oh." Momma unwrapped her sandwich and took a bite. "I hadn't really thought about it."

"You want to rent it, right?"

"Yeah, that's what I'm thinking."

"'Cause this place is like, paid off."

"Right," Momma mumbled through a mouthful of peanut butter.

It made Caroline uncomfortable to be alone with

Grandma's Way

Momma at the table, with no TV to distract them like at home. All Momma's country ways came out when they were alone. If anyone else in the universe was sitting at Grandma's table, Momma would not have crumbs covering her T-shirt or jelly in the corner of her mouth.

"So what is the first thing you're gonna do with that money?"

Caroline knew exactly what Momma was going to do—fix up their house, because that was an *investment*, and still continue to save every fucking nickel she could. So Caroline didn't have to *really* listen to Momma's plans.

But she pretended to. Momma didn't have a whole lot of friends, and the ones she had she didn't trust. Caroline knew her momma was lonely and also not the brightest light bulb on the planet.

All Caroline had to do was interject comments from time to time, such as, "really?" or repeat the last thing her momma said, "So you want to paint the living room blue?"

Caroline held back from saying things like, "The living room is on the *north* side of the house, and if you paint it *blue* it will be *gloomier* than ever."

Her plan worked. Momma relaxed and got animated. "And once the house is done, maybe I'll even get a new car," which Caroline knew meant another used vehicle, just not as old or as horribly embarrassing as the green station wagon. But what Caroline said was, "You know what? I don't see how this could go wrong. You've really thought this through, Momma." She almost felt guilty about the big grin plastered on her mother's face. "I mean, really. Someone else probably would have sold it and lost the money in the stock market, or something." Saying this, Caroline realized it was also true.

Momma leaned forward, as if telling a secret. "I thought about it, but the realtors I spoke to gave me such low prices on the place, and what if later on the area gets built up?"

Caroline smiled. "You're thinking long term. That's the smart thing. Good for you, Momma. A lot of these old neighborhoods get going again."

"Well, I guess we'll see." Momma looked at her watch. "Oh, my gosh, it's after one."

"Are you working today?"

"Yes, and I've got to get cleaned up." Momma stood, stretching and arching her back like it hurt.

Caroline panicked. "Well, wait a minute. How about making a deal with me?"

"About what?"

"About the dance."

"Caroline, I already told you—"

"Hear me out. What time are you getting off?"

"Nine."

"Okay, here's my proposition. I finish the attic while you're at work today and be here tomorrow, and after school every day. I'll paint and wax the floors and everything, even weekends until it's finished. It could be done by the end of November. We could rent it out in December."

That was the punch line. Caroline held her breath while dangling all that money coming in so soon. Momma hadn't considered it a possibility.

"Well, I don't know."

Caroline knew it would take some time of pondering before Momma would make a decision, but an outright "no" had been avoided, and her pulse quickened.

Caroline pointed at the box. "I can do this. I can tell what's good and what's junk." That was the second carrot. Offering to use her brains to assist Momma in things Momma wasn't too sure about.

"And you'd really help? Even after the dance?"

"Cross my heart and hope to die."

"And you'll pull up geometry."

"I'll buckle down, I promise." Buckling down was something Momma was always telling her to do.

Momma nodded, considering. "I'll think about it.

What about your costume? Isn't it at the house?"

"Yeah, but I can find something here. I could wear a housecoat of Grandma's and go as an old lady." Caroline smiled, sure the wind was blowing her way. "I can take a shower here, and stuff."

"I'll think about it. I'll call you later."

"I don't have a phone, remember?"

"Just haul an upstairs phone out into the hallway." Momma stood up and switched off the window air conditioner.

To Caroline the silence made the kitchen feel dead, oppressive. But Momma didn't notice, looking for car keys in her pocketbook. Watching, Caroline wondered if Momma ever felt a damn thing. Grandma's death was not even a blip on her radar, although she put on a good act at the funeral. But Momma had always been like a robot, focused on work at home and at her job, squeezing the shit out of any nickel that came her way and watching that damned bank account grow. Shaking her head, Caroline displaced gloomy thoughts of dead things and people who didn't feel anything.

"I'll call before eight."

Caroline walked Momma to the front door, trying to ensure her thoughts stayed positive. She even smiled, leaned in and gave Momma a semi-hug when kissed goodbye. And then went back to the kitchen to collect

Grandma's Way

the coveted tin box.

Caroline found another tin box among the others she'd brought down, shaped like the one she wanted. After washing it, and putting it where the other had been on the counter, she got the one she wanted, a roll of packing tape, and went down the basement steps.

Down there wasn't as icy as the kitchen, but cooler than the rest of the house, and still had the damp smell she'd always loved.

When she was little, and they were living with Grandma, Daddy had made a play area for her in the corner of the basement, under the one window that got some light. He'd gotten the small metal kitchen set at a yard sale, or somewhere. Caroline put her tin box in the small oven part of the stove; it barely fit. She taped the oven door shut. She'd told Momma she wanted to keep the set for her own kids, a total lie because Caroline never intended to have children. She just wanted to keep the only thing Daddy had given her before he got sick of Momma and left.

Despite the unwanted second sandwich, Caroline felt hollow inside, looking around the basement already emptied of old clothes, old furniture, broken electric fans, TVs, and other junk Momma had gotten the thrift store to haul away.

Only the washer and dryer on the opposite wall, the

copper pipes running the length of the ceiling, the drain in the floor, and her kitchen set were where they had always been. Caroline sighed and dejectedly went up the steps to the kitchen.

Even more reluctantly, she left the kitchen, still chilly in its silence.

Grandma's bedroom was in the front of the house. It was the biggest bedroom and the nicest by far. It was the only room in the house still looking the way Grandma left it. All the other bedrooms had been stripped of curtains and bedding, but Grandma's brass bed still had its cheerful pink and blue quilt. Grandma's pink wall-to-wall carpeting felt good underfoot as Caroline came in and flopped on the bed, dialing a number on Grandma's fake antique gold phone, glad there was no way Momma could trace the call.

"Mandy?"

"Yeah?"

"It's me, Caroline."

"Oh, hey there, how's it going?"

"Awful. Well. . ." Caroline considered her situation. "Actually, not too bad. I think I got her talked into letting me go."

"That's great. How'd you do it?"

Caroline complained about Momma constantly, but she was only like every other fifteen-year-old girl in her school. Yet for reasons foggy, and unclear, Caroline never bitched about things seriously wrong with Momma, like being stupid. "Oh, I promised to do better. I told her I was still upset about Grandma."

"And she bought that?" Mandy shrieked.

"Well, we *were* pretty close."

"When? You hated going over there."

"She was old then, and sick."

"So you were close when you were little?"

"Sort of. Not like gushy close. We were more alike than close, I guess."

"Whatever, Caroline. At least your momma is letting you go."

"Right." Caroline had no idea what in the hell she was trying to say. "So anyway, can you bring the cat costume?"

"Oh, yeah, I forgot about that. Sure, I will."

"And some heels?"

"You want to wear my shoes?"

"Yeah, mine are at home."

"That's right, you're at your grandma's. What size do you wear?"

"Seven."

"I wear a six. Mine won't fit and I don't want you to stretch them out." Mandy added, "Sorry," but she sounded like she didn't much care.

Caroline desperately thought about alternative footwear. She *had* to have heels. Black ones like the spikes hidden in her closet at home. Damn Mandy for being such a picky bitch.

"Well, just bring the costume then, and I'll figure something out."

"Okay, I've got to go. Mom's dragging us all out to lunch." Mandy groaned, like going to a *restaurant* was a chore.

"Okay, thanks, bye." Caroline hung up, rolled over and stretched out on the bed, staring at the ceiling fan, and regretting not having turned it on.

She pictured what Mandy was doing, going through her parents' sunny home, her two little brothers bouncing down the stairs, all of them piling into their cool SUV and going somewhere nice.

Probably a restaurant that even had cloth napkins. The hollow feeling in her stomach got worse.

Shaking off all the crap that liked to occupy her head, Caroline sat up. Directly across from the bed was Grandma's huge closet. She'd turned Caroline's old bedroom into a sliver of its former self when she had her double side-by-side closet put in.

Caroline opened all the louvered doors. Shoe boxes, probably fifty of them, were stacked on the short side wall on the left. Pushing the clothing on the rack to the middle, Caroline turned and slid down the back wall until she was sitting. Maybe she'd get lucky.

Pulling out shoeboxes from the bottom of the stacks wasn't easy. She had to keep the upper boxes from becoming dislodged, but she knew her grandma well enough to know the oldest shoes were at the bottom.

And they would have to be very old, to be remotely what Caroline was looking for.

The first pair were so old, Caroline wasn't sure they were even Grandma's. Open-toed beige heels made of leather, each decorated with a big leather beige rose, and two green leather leaves. Caroline shook her head with wonder. The vintage shop would love them.

She opened more boxes and found more fancy shoes, some made of clear vinyl, now cracked, instead of leather. Others were made of flowered fabric and other fabric heels dyed to match some dress Grandma probably still had hanging in the closet. But no spikes of any kind, and the shoes were getting newer and older at once; the high heels becoming medium heels, the colors becoming sedate browns, blacks, and tans. Caroline sighed, feeling unlucky as hell.

But the next box surprised her with its lightness. She shook it; something was in there, but not shoes.

Caroline pulled out a packet of insurance policies.

At first she was excited by the find, thinking Grandma had gotten some life insurance after all. The thought of presenting some windfall to Momma, and the glory that would follow, filled Caroline's mind. But as she opened and flipped through the brittle pages she found Imogene Walker, Imogene Peterson, Imogene Jenkins, and Imogene Porter the recipient of all those policies.

Caroline smiled. Each policy was nearly double the previous. The last one on Grandpa Porter had been for a hundred thousand dollars, and it suddenly struck her as odd to find them there, hidden in the multitude of shoes. And all that money—*damn, a hundred thousand dollars paid out less than ten years ago. How much money had Momma inherited?*

Not that it mattered. She now knew, no amount was enough. And it wasn't likely she'd ever see a nickel of it, Momma being only seventeen years older than her daughter. Even if Momma did kick the bucket first, Caroline would probably be too old to enjoy it. *Nobody will ever have fun with any of that money.*

She picked up and shook all the boxes that were left unopened, opened a few but found nothing else interesting. The dyed, black silk, medium-high heels she'd put aside would have to do. It was a shame; the cat costume was made for spikes. Caroline tried them on and looked in the full-length mirror. Hardly even medium height. Turning, she pictured herself in the costume with Grandma's dinky heels and wondered how she was supposed to survive the never-ending scraping of shit together and all the making-do that was her life. Putting her flip-flops back on, she restacked the shoes, putting the insurance policies box back in the middle where they'd been, and wondering why.

A glance at the clock on Grandma's nightstand startled her with its lateness. Caroline rummaged through Grandma's closet and quickly located an old-lady dress that would work with the heels, a really sick hat, big-brimmed and awful, and lots of crappy jewelry from Grandma's dresser. She left everything on Grandma's bed for later on.

If everything went as planned, when Momma dropped her off at school that night she would smile fondly at the get-up she thought her daughter was wearing that evening. She didn't know Caroline kept a full arsenal of makeup in her locker.

Momma didn't have a clue about so many things it boggled Caroline's mind from time to time.

Leaving Grandma's room, Caroline went down the hall to the back staircase and up to the attic, which was even hotter with late afternoon sun streaming through the front window.

Turning in a circle, she gauged what needed to

happen in the next five hours. She actually could do what she promised because Grandma had taught her. "I'll pay you top dollar, just like I pay Otis," Grandma had said, pointing a perfectly manicured pink fingernail at her. "And you aren't nearly as strong as Otis, but you are, at least, a whole lot smarter." Grandma scowled, shaking her hand, diamonds flashing from gnarled fingers. "But if I catch you slacking off for one minute, I'll get Otis back here before you can blink an eye. And if I do," Grandma leaned in to let Caroline know she meant it, "I'll never hire you again, even if I have to stand beside Otis all day long so he knows what to do next."

Caroline believed her, and had paid attention and learned how to do the spring cleaning, the gardening, how to paint rooms and kitchen cabinets, even how to refinish furniture. Which was how she earned the money to buy the phone Momma took away whenever she felt like it.

She started with the other long, low shelf running under the eaves, one glance telling her it was mostly garbage. She wasted a few minutes looking for something to hold the trash bags, before figuring out an upturned wooden bar stool did the trick. The shelf filled three plastic bags with glass jars once holding spaghetti sauce, or pickles, boxes of ancient bills and check stubs, two toasters so old their cords were made of some kind of frayed fabric, and other useless junk. The glass jars exploded when the bags hit the sidewalk, sounding great even from way up here.

Old oil lamps from the shelf filled two cardboard boxes, because Caroline had to pad them with newspapers. She carried the boxes downstairs and ran back up. She knew the more boxes waiting to greet Momma when she got back, the better.

The bureau was crammed with old stuff which she boxed and carried downstairs.

Other boxes followed as she dismantled areas piled with old furniture, rugs, tablecloths and framed paintings and photos.

Some ornate wicker furniture stacked in the corner, so fried from heat the pieces were light as feathers and too brittle to be used, were dropped from the window. They exploded when hitting the sidewalk, but it was a silent and unsatisfying explosion.

Near the front, Caroline found two sewing machines she didn't remember Grandma having, a bunch of old patterns, and some fabric. Caroline carried those and four old washboards down the two flights of stairs.

She dragged an empty steamer trunk down the attic steps, but left it in the upstairs hallway. She couldn't lift it for long, and it would scratch up the floor if she dragged it farther.

Her hair was soaking, as were her shirt and underwear. After carrying down more boxes, she stopped off in the kitchen, still cool and dim. Caroline drank an entire bottle of water from the cooler, now deliciously cold, and tasting better than anything she'd had in a while.

She used the sprayer on the sink to soak her hair with cold water. It felt wonderful too. She checked the clock. She still had two hours to get it all done. Grabbing another water bottle, she went back up.

Wicker laundry baskets, still in decent shape, were filled with quilts, blankets and old bedspreads. Caroline recognized the one from her bed when she was five, and patted the sun-bonneted little-girl appliqué she remembered so well. But it was bundled up and carried down along with the others. Her pile was getting impressive—rolled-up rugs balanced on different-sized boxes, lamps, a coffee table, two modern-looking wood chairs with faded gray cushions, and probably twenty large boxes of things. Caroline grabbed a stepstool from the kitchen and went back to the attic.

The last big item to deal with was the huge shelf built into the back wall, under the high windows. Using the stepstool, Caroline still had to reach to get at the dust-covered copper molds on top of the shelf. She dropped them on a green wool blanket she'd put on the floor. She got all she could reach, knowing Momma would never spot the ones left, and moved down to the top shelf.

The shelves were deep, probably eighteen inches, and all five feet of length packed with old salt shakers, pitchers, mixing bowls—most of them some kind of ceramic, or glass, and all of them requiring wrapping in newspaper—boxed, and carried downstairs. It took almost the full two hours to finish two shelves.

She wiped the sweat stinging her eyes with her T-shirt. Despite the impressive amount of things downstairs, the monstrous shelf might be her undoing. She got less picky, brought over her upturned barstool/garbage-bag system and began tossing in glasses that probably weren't worth anything, mismatched plates, and dented aluminum bowls, then tied the bags and tossed them out the window. Lovely smashing followed.

Rushing through the next two shelves, carrying down only one more box of things she'd given a second thought to, she found the light getting dim and turned on the glaring naked bulbs in the attic's rafters.

The bottom shelf, the worst one because she had to get on her hands and knees to get to it, was last. Only inches off the floor, she bent to peer at the collection of jars that resided there.

They were odd looking at first, until she figured out they were ancient glass canning jars with wires that clamped their glass lids to them. Even covered in dust, she could tell some were clear glass while others were a pretty aqua. Tiny jars in the front to large ones in the back filled the shelf. Caroline pulled one out and sat up to inspect it. She worked out how to unlatch the glass top, but it wouldn't come off.

Using the handle of a metal spoon that missed the trash bag, she pried off the lid and found some kind of melting rubber seal gripping the top to the jar. She touched it, and was reminded of the melting rubber-band ball.

Bending to see if they were all that way, the best as she could tell in the dark under there, they were.

And she knew *exactly* who would be cleaning the damned gunk off all those jars, if she were to pull them out, wrap them, not get the shelf done, risk pissing off Momma, et cetera, et cetera, et cetera.

Caroline grabbed a plastic bag and began shoving in glass containers. Once it was half full, she gathered up garbage in the room to add to the bag—old magazines and bills, rags—in case Momma opened a bag to check what was in it.

Grandma's Way

It made the loudest crash of all, as did the next two. She took a break to drink some water. It wouldn't do to have a heat stroke and not be able to go to the dance after all. She looked around the mostly empty attic, knowing Momma would be pleased.

Getting on her belly to fish out the last jars in the back of shelf, she found behind one of them, a small, ancient, amber bottle with a cork stopper. She pulled the tiny thing out, wondering, *What the hell?*

She stood, then took the squat jar still holding a dark, thick liquid to the front windows to better see its label. The sun was setting, the tree no longer blazing and reflecting red in the attic, but when she held the small bottle to the waning light, the word *Poison* jumped out at her.

Why would Grandma have hidden it there?

At first it was an innocent question, but Grandma's four husbands and those four hidden insurance policies invaded her mind, the kind of invasion she couldn't shake off, and despite the heat, sweat, and dust clinging to her body, a deep chill moved through her.

She knew Grandma's last two husbands both left her with good pensions.

The old bag never worked one day in her life, bragged about it even. And she'd always enjoyed herself, even if she had been half-crazy and selfish as hell.

Whenever Momma disapproved of something Caroline did, she'd say, "I swear, you are *exactly* like your grandma, and not in a good way." Then Momma would sigh and continue believing it wasn't *her* fault her daughter had so many problems.

A phone began ringing, echoing in the empty hallway downstairs as Caroline slipped the bottle in the back pocket of her jeans. Racing to answer the phone, she smiled at the thought.

Maybe Momma got one thing right after all.

Grandma's Way

Blood Moon

by

Leah St. James

Chapter One

On the beach, two lovers kissed. Behind them, the moon—hanging giant and hazy red in the sky—dripped feathery tendrils into the sea, painting crimson tips on the dancing waves.

Its raw beauty was lost on the two, engrossed as they were in each other, entwined so closely, they appeared from a distance as one. They never heard my approach. Never knew I'd been observing them earlier while they joined their friends around a bonfire.

I moved closer, my steps inaudible over the crashing surf. Something about the woman—girl really—called to me. More than that...vexed me.

Maybe it was her waist-length hair the color of coal. Most of the girls teased their hair into those ugly beehives, but she'd let hers flow free, like a curtain of silk. She reminded me of...

I forced that image from my mind. Maybe it was the way her date, a handsome young man, brought her hand to his mouth for a kiss. He pressed his lips not to the back of her hand, like a gentleman would, but to the center of her palm. I imagined their eyes making love as surely as if they lay together, unclothed, in bed.

Maybe it was her response, a trill of sensuous laughter, carried by the sea-scented breezes to my ears.

My stomach stormed. What made her boy-man so special? Why did he deserve her love?

A need to make her suffer, just as I had suffered, rose and filled my soul with hate. Despite that, my hands flexed with the urge to touch, to sample the woman's lushness, the curves so happily on display in the indecently short dress with fanciful red polka dots that looked eerily like that moon.

Was it a symbol, a sign, that it was time to indulge that craving for her body, her blood? Was it destiny that brought me to their part of the world on that specific night?

I moved in. First on the boyfriend. So unaware. So full of youthful passion in the way he clutched her close. A quick chop to the back of the head, and the boy-man was down, twitching in the sand. When he woke, would he understand that it was his attention that caused her death?

I turned to her. She backed up, her eyes rounded, her hands over her open mouth. Screams bubbled from her crimson lips, so loud and shrill they must have come from some deep dark place in her soul.

Blood coursed through my veins, carried by the excitement of the prize before me, and I laughed at the sheer power of the moment. I stepped closer, close enough to see that her cheeks were wet with tears, close enough to smell fear.

I grabbed for her and —

Something hot and sweaty clamped on the back of Ronnie's neck, and a shriek tore up her throat as she twisted to face her attacker.

Matthew jumped back, hands lifted, palms out. "What the hell, Ronnie? I just wanted to tell you it's almost time to go."

"Sorry." Sitting up from where she'd been lounging on the couch, she gave her husband a sheepish smile and drew in a slow breath to calm her heart. "I was reading." She flipped the paperback around to show him the cover of the true-crime novel she'd started earlier in the day.

Half illustration, half black-and-white photo, it depicted a shadowed man poised over a woman sprawled on a beach. Her body lay prone, right arm akimbo, legs splayed. A tear in the bodice of her mini-dress revealed a jagged, bloody gash over her heart. Blood had gushed from the wound and pooled in the sand at her side, puddled slick and oily-looking in a splash of red moonlight. In the background, a man's face stared from behind prison bars with eyes that were at once triumphant and defiant.

It was a mock-up—he'd never been caught—but every time Ronnie looked at the cover, she shivered at the sheer evil of the man whose very real kill diary had been excerpted in the best-seller.

With a snort, Matthew took the paperback, flipped her bookmark in place, then snapped it shut and placed it on the end table. "What a shock. I'm surprised you even remember you have a real life half the time. Pretty soon you're going to be buried in your work...literally." He gestured to the several stacks of books crawling drunkenly up the wall in the corner of their living room.

"Not all of us can have jobs saving the world," she said, raising her voice so he could hear her as he walked away. Wasn't a big to-be-read pile to be expected for the life of a book reviewer?

Besides, it was her fascination with crime that had drawn her to him in the first place. They'd met at a mystery readers' conference. He'd presented a talk about profiling serial killers, and she'd spent most of the time watching how his hands worked the laser pointer and how his eyes rested on each individual in the audience, as if cataloging them. When they met hers, something electric sizzled through her veins. Smitten, she'd gone up to him afterward, introduced herself and asked to see his badge.

As pick-up lines went, it might have been cheesy, but they'd been together since.

Smiling at the memory, Ronnie moved into the kitchen to gather their contributions to the Halloween party their best friends were hosting that evening. While half her mind focused on the tapas tray she'd prepared, the other half refused to leave the moonlit beach... refused to leave the young lovers in the hands of the psychopathic killer who'd been hunted by police for weeks before the trail had turned cold.

Dubbed the "Harvest Moon Slasher" back then, the man had terrorized a ten-mile stretch of beach in a five-hour period, claiming more than a dozen lives one late October evening fifty years ago. All women. All with young men who were curiously left injured, but alive. Before the attacks, the couples had been living their lives, unaware they'd be forever changed before the sun rose. Some were attending Halloween parties at the beach. Some a dance at the local college. Others just out for a stroll in the moonlight.

The women had all been found in the sand with a circle shape carved over the heart. A sharp-witted investigator had finally figured out it was a sign for the full moon that had been hanging big and red in the sky that night.

As Ronnie headed upstairs to get ready, she shook her head free of the image of blood flowing over the heroine's pretty sundress, trying not to think how weirdly similar it was to the costume she'd chosen for the evening.

Matthew had beaten her to their bedroom and was getting dressed in his Ivy Leaguer costume of classic pleated trousers in khaki and a mock turtleneck in navy blue. The real star of the costume, though, was the winter white button-down cardigan with the big blue "B" on the left chest. A set of matching stripes circled the left bicep, and the number "60" had been embroidered in the center. His grandfather's prized letterman sweater, discovered only recently in the attic, had been the inspiration for their theme of young, hip 1960s couple in love.

As she crossed the threshold, the scent of something spicy and woodsy tickled her nose. "What is that smell?" She moved next to him and sniffed. "Are you wearing cologne? You never wear cologne."

"I know, but apparently my grandfather did." He held up a small, rectangular bottle with a spritzer top and a Western-style label with a lasso logo. "I was poking around in the attic, looking for shoes to go with this get-up, and found another box of his stuff, including this." He pumped the top, and Ronnie stepped back before the spray could hit her.

"Don't let it touch your skin. It's ancient."

He snorted. "I ain't afraid of no sissy perfume."

"Yeah, well, when you break out in hives, you'll wish you'd listened."

"Just hand me the sweater, will you? We're late."

She reached for the sweater where it lay on the bed and absently shook it out, releasing the cedar-y scent of the chest where it had lain, as if freeing spirits trapped in the yarn.

Matthew took it from her and slipped it on, then spread his arms and glanced down at himself. "How stupid do I look?"

"Not stupid at all. Collegiately handsome. Just like him, actually."

Grandpa Tom, as Matt referred to him, had died when Matt was a toddler. Matt told no touching stories of grandfatherly wisdoms shared. But his ancestor's life had been painted in the photos they'd found in the attic, dropped loosely in old boxes like shoes that needed new soles but no one left to wear them.

Lifeguard Tom surrounded by an assortment of giggling girls at the beach, posing like Mr. Universe, hands on his swimsuit-briefed hips, a come-and-get-me grin on his face.

Letterman Tom in college, wearing the sweater and holding a football with his arm cranked back, preparing to Hail Mary the ball to the end zone.

Graduate Tom in his cap and gown, looking steadily but fiercely into the camera, eager to tackle the world.

Another with a young woman at what looked like a college dance—maybe for a fraternity or sorority. She wore a cocktail dress in pale pink; he wore a slimly tailored suit. They looked in love. Ronnie had always wondered who she was.

The photos progressed, telling tales of his marriage, family man and fatherhood to a boy and girl—Matt's uncle and mother—and finally as grandfather to Matthew and his older cousin, posing in front of a Christmas tree.

Sometimes Ronnie couldn't help but wonder if Tom's spirit roamed the beach house that he and Matthew's grandmother had built as newlyweds. She had no proof, just a feeling of something—a spirit—nearby, one that was neither benevolent nor malevolent. Just...

there, as if watching.

He'd been a local cop, his wife a teacher, and the two had built the house as a summer retreat, then added on and moved in full time when their family grew. His wife had died first, and when he died, Tom left the home to Matthew's mother, who in turn had rented it for years before transferring title to Matthew and Ronnie a year earlier.

Ronnie had always wondered why her mother-in-law hadn't returned to her childhood home on the spit of beachfront near the Virginia/North Carolina border. Such a prized location. Even with its history of death.

"I'll see you downstairs."

Jolting at the sound of her husband's voice, she blinked. He stood in the doorway, one eyebrow lifted.

"Yes. I'll be right down."

Hurrying, she pulled her costume from her closet. She'd found the cocktail dress at a vintage store in Richmond. The strapless under-dress with a sweetheart neckline was white with red polka dots, and a sleeveless overdress of white chiffon floated on top. She'd found a wide strip of crimson satin to match the dots and wrapped it around her waist, tying it into a big bow at the back.

She moved into the bathroom to fix her hair, intending to tease it into a beehive at the back, then roll the rest into a sleek French twist. But Matthew was waiting, so she ran a brush through the length, settling for a quick tease near the crown—as was the fashion back then—and finished it off with a white headband with red polka dots, a dollar-store find. She slipped her feet into the pair of kitten-heeled Capezios in the softest kid leather that at some point had been dyed a blood red.

There was that word again. Blood. It wouldn't go away.

Chapter Two

Outside, the sea breezes gusted, sending a chill across Ronnie's bare shoulders, and she wrapped her arms around herself to rub some warmth into them.

"Here, take this." Matthew handed her the tapas dish while he started to shrug out of the sweater.

"No." She stopped him with a hand on his shoulder. "I'll be fine once we're inside." She stroked her hand along the fabric. "You look so cute. I can see why your grandmother fell in love with your grandfather."

He stopped, slid his free arm around her waist and drew her to his side. "Yeah?"

"Yeah."

"Maybe we should head back home. George and Tina won't care—"

"Don't even think it. They're our best friends. Tina would never forgive me if we skipped their party."

"Even if she knew how we were spending the time instead?" He nuzzled her neck, his voice going all deep and husky, and for a moment Ronnie let the warm gush of love tempt her.

But when the picture of her friend, scowling and shaking a scolding finger, erupted in Ronnie's head, she stepped to the side, away from Matthew's touch. "Especially if she knew I was getting lucky while she was dealing with 'Crazy Gus' all by herself."

It was a nickname they'd given to a neighbor, an elderly man whose wife, Annie, had disappeared several decades earlier. He'd reported her missing hours after leaving a party at a local club, saying she'd complained about an old boyfriend bothering her in the days before her disappearance. When the local police responded, they found a Dear John note in the den—and a medicine chest full of anxiety meds in the bathroom cabinet. They questioned the ex-boyfriend, even searched his house, but nothing was ever discovered that tied the two of them together, other than Gus's statement.

Without a body or evidence of foul play, the cops closed the investigation almost before it was opened. Still, Gus considered his wife dead and every so often he'd pester the cops to reopen the case.

He pleaded with Matthew from time to time, and had given him a file he'd compiled at the time of the disappearance—lists of suspects, a timeline, theories on why someone would kill his wife. It was surprisingly thick, and Matthew had been impressed with Gus's diligence and attention to detail. A few months back, he'd even interviewed the few residents of the block who'd been around back then. But there was still nothing there. Still no body. Still no reason to believe Gus's wife hadn't simply run off to live the good life with a new man.

When Ronnie had first heard about him, she felt bad for the old guy, until he'd cornered her one time while she was out for a run, telling her he saw spirits around her. She'd spent the rest of the run jogging backward more than forward. It had taken her weeks to shake the feeling. Even now when she went out alone, that episode would pop to the front of her mind. Her skin would prickle and she'd have to do mental gymnastics to erase the sensation.

Otherwise Gus seemed harmless. He had the best Christmas decorations on the street—telling those who asked that he wanted the lights bright enough for his wife to see in heaven. And every Halloween, he left a giant tub of sweets and toys on his front stoop for the neighborhood kids to take. Bad guys didn't do things like that...unless they wanted to lure the innocent.

Ronnie shook away the ridiculous thought. Aside from the occasional creepy episode, Gus wasn't a bad guy. After all, who wouldn't go a little crazy if deserted by a spouse who had promised to stick with you, through good and bad?

That was the consensus of the group of neighbors on the block anyway, and individually they tried to include Gus in neighborhood events whenever possible. Still, Ronnie and Tina had made a pact to always have each other's back around him, and Ronnie wasn't about to break that promise, even in a house overflowing with partiers.

"No, I can't stand her up," she repeated, giving her husband an apologetic smile.

Resigned, Matthew took her hand, planted a kiss on her knuckles, and let her tug him toward their friend's home a few doors down.

****

One of the larger homes on the narrow spit of land, the house rose three stories high, with decks on the first two levels and a small balcony on the third, adding even more space for the neighbors who had spilled out of every opening, like mud through fence slats.

Guests—dressed in an assortment of costumes from ghoulish to eye-popping sensual, drinks and plates in hand—leaned in to hear each other over the Grateful Dead singing about friends and devils. Tempted to slap her hands over her ears to dull the din, Ronnie plunged into the action.

She spotted George and Tina within the first minute. They'd dressed as Count and Countess Dracula. Tina's home-designed outfit was a cross between Eddie Munster and Elvira, with a gleaming fall of fake black hair that reached almost to her butt.

After a quick check-in—accomplished with a brief hug and air kisses—Ronnie and Matthew wormed their way to the food tables.

She squeezed her tapas tray into a spot between a platter of cheese and crackers and a pot of Swedish meatballs, then grabbed plates. She tipped her head toward the end of the table where chafing dishes warmed the main courses. "I'm starved."

Matthew stayed close at her rear as they jostled their way to the end of the main serving line. Directly in front of them, a couple talked quietly to each other. The woman, a brassy blonde with enough face makeup to mask whatever her age, had dressed in a red-and-black striped knit dress, black knee-high boots with buckles and zippers, and a brown felt hat. A female version of Freddy Krueger. She caught Ronnie's eye and nodded a hello.

"I didn't know there'd be so many of y'all here." Her accent pegged her from the Deep South. She peeked around her partner's bulk. Tall—well over six feet—he had dressed as the nightmare man himself. Both wore flesh-colored gloves with the nails...claws... things on the end.

"It's the biggest party of the year, in our little neighborhood anyway." Ronnie glanced around at the increasingly diminishing free space. "Last year Tina—that's the hostess—counted just over a hundred people."

"Good thing there's enough food to feed a couple high school football teams," the wife said. "I'm Barbara. We just moved into the house at the end. This is my husband, Fred."

"Seriously?" Ronnie craned her neck so she could focus on the man's face...mask. "Your name really is Fred?"

"Yeah," the guy said with a laugh. "Is that a problem?" His voice was Darth Vader deep but accented like a Highlander.

"No! Of course not. I just..." At a loss for words, she glanced at the wife. She was making faces at her husband behind his back. "It makes perfect sense."

"The costume was my idea." Barbara said, flapping her hand in a "whatever" gesture. "I thought it would be fun. But poor Fred is burning up under that awful mask.

And these hands," she lifted one of her paws, displaying the blade-like extensions as if she were showing off a new manicure, "are not user friendly."

"Yeah, they look...difficult. Unless you have to kill your meal with your bare hands." Ronnie squinted again. "They look amazingly real. Do you mind..." She pointed, and when the woman nodded, she gripped and discovered a very human hand under the fake layer of rubber-tipped claws. Relieved, she let a chuckle slip out.

"That's what I get for reading a true murder story before heading to a Halloween party," she said with a shake of her head. "I'm Ronnie, and this is my husband, Matthew."

Matthew nodded to the man. "Good to meet you."

He was eyeing the guy in that way men have of sizing each other up. Apparently meeting the challenge, Fred grabbed the top of the mask with his claw hand and tugged. When it popped free with a *snap!*, he handed it to his wife. With a grimace, she tucked it into the tote-sized purse hanging from her shoulder.

Fred wiped his forearm along his brow where his dark hair, a shade shy of black, had curled with the sweat. Then he offered his hand to Matthew. "And you as well."

He looked older than she'd imagined—maybe

early fifties judging by the lines that marked the corners of his mouth and the silver shooting through his hair. The eyes were dark, too, his gaze intense, like he was looking deeper than called for by a casual introduction. Like Matthew.

"Where you from?"

"Ah, you picked up on my accent." A smile lifted the corners of Fred's mouth. Without answering, he moved down the row of food, filling his plate.

"Well, yeah. From the U.K.?"

"Actually, American born, just raised in the U.K."

"Really." Matthew stepped around Ronnie and followed the couple to a table on the deck.

Ronnie took a seat next to Matthew. "So why did you leave?" When Fred's eyebrows lifted, she pressed her hand over her mouth. "I'm sorry, that was rude. I'm a sucker for people's stories."

"No harm," Fred said easily with another half-smile. "I have no secrets. My parents died when I was an infant. Da was from the U.K. One of his sisters took me home to live with her family in Northumberland. That's where I was raised. Thus the accent." He lifted his hands up, palms out. "See? No mystery."

"No, but sad. I'm sorry."

When he didn't answer, Matthew said, "I'm not familiar with Northumberland."

"Northeast, on the coast up by the Scottish border. Nothing but land for miles around. Pretty land, fantastic medieval castles and coal mines."

Something tickled Ronnie's memory at the last, but it disappeared before she could decipher it. "Sounds intriguing."

He made a noncommittal humming noise, and she followed his gaze to the beach below where the party had spilled from the house. Someone had built a bonfire to roast marshmallows, and a few guests had run to the water line to wet their feet.

When she looked up, she found him staring at her, sipping from his bottle, and she jerked a fraction before controlling it. "So how did you end up back here, in the U.S.?"

"Went to university here. I wanted to experience my birth country. Got a scholarship to play football—" He lifted his bottle in a silent salute. "The real football. You call it soccer."

"Yeah, yeah...whatever," she said with a roll of her eyes, then fixed her gaze on Barbara. "How did you two meet?"

"She's my realtor. She sold me my house. We hit it off."

"No kidding." Matthew, who had been staring at the couple, zeroed in on the wife. "I thought you looked familiar. I've seen your ads in the paper. You're the 'bring me any deal and I'll make it work' person."

"That's right." Barbara sat up and smoothed a hand over her hair. "I was so happy we were able to negotiate a settlement for the house. It meant so much to Fred."

"Oh?" Matthew had been packing away cole slaw and pulled pork, but put his fork down and pushed his chair back an inch. "Where did you buy?"

"His mama and daddy's house, that little cottage around the bend at the end of the road. He'd contacted me all the way from England to ask about purchasing."

"Really." Matthew turned to Fred. "What kind of work do you do?"

Ronnie knew what he was thinking. The house was small, but situated on a knuckle of oceanfront land about half an acre from the roadway. The property was probably worth close to a million dollars. That was a lot of money, and a long way to travel, for childhood nostalgia.

"Matt," Ronnie said, grabbing her husband's arm, "stop giving him the third degree. We're at a party."

"Asking a man's line of work is not the third degree." There was a tone of finality in his answer that she was about to challenge when Fred responded.

"No harm. I'm in securities. I took a transfer here and had a yearning for the house my parents shared.

Barb helped me broker a deal with the owners. And here we are." He saluted with his bottle, then laughed, a sudden burst that had a crazed tone to it. Then he took another swig of beer, as if to stifle himself.

Matthew might have questioned him more if George hadn't stopped by their table at that moment. After a few minutes of small talk, he jerked his thumb toward the back of the house. "Mind taking a turn at the grill?"

Groaning, Matthew stood. "I did promise, didn't I?"

"I'll come with you." Ronnie hated to admit it, but the Freddy Krueger costumes were giving her the creeps.

As they moved toward the grill area, Ronnie pulled next to George. "The new neighbors seem nice."

"Hmm..."

"What? What does that 'hmm' mean?"

"Nothing. It doesn't mean a thing. They seem nice. What you said."

It was a very un-George like thing to say. "Nice" wasn't usually in his vocabulary, it was too vague. George was the type of guy who would tell you in plain language what he thought, whether or not you wanted to hear it. Ronnie looked behind them to see several people had taken their places at the table. Her gaze darted back to George. His eyes were narrowed on the couple like he expected them to stuff his silverware down their shirts.

"You know," she said, tugging on his sleeve, "just because you own one of the biggest security firms in the mid-Atlantic doesn't mean everyone you meet is a suspect."

He snickered, not a pleasant sound, his eyes trained on Fred and Barbara for another count of five before he dropped the pose and met her gaze. "Who said anything about suspecting them of anything? I've invited them into my home, haven't I?"

Matthew made a rude noise.

"And you," Ronnie said, stabbing his chest with her finger, "just because your job has you on call 24/7 doesn't mean you can't let down your guard for a nano-second."

"That's one theory," he said, but his eyes locked with George's, and some sort of male communication passed between them as clearly as if cartoon bubbles suspended over their heads. Unfortunately, the ink was invisible.

"You know I hate when you two do that silent talking thing." Ignoring their fake protestations of innocence, she grabbed her plate and pointed it toward the upper deck where Tina had been holding court. "I'm going to find Tina," she said with a final nod to her husband.

As she passed through the main party area on her way outside, she glanced to Fred...whoever, wishing she'd asked the couple's real last name. He was laughing as he brought a longneck bottle of beer to his mouth. Barbara sat next to him, a goblet of what looked like white wine in her hand—sans the paw—and was talking with giant gestures. Already the two fit right in with their little group.

Unsure why it gave her a twinge of...something, Ronnie shook off the sensation and pushed through the kitchen, crowded with yet more people, and out to the deck where someone had cranked up a stereo in the hopes of competing with the roar of the tide. It was near its lowest point for the day, but the surf was up, remnants of a nasty nor'easter that had pummeled the coast a few days earlier, and a few brave surfers rode the waves in the waning light.

On the beach, families were packing up, heading home to wash off layers of sand, sea salt and SPF-whatever protection. A gust of wind brought the cries of a reluctant toddler from near the water's edge. His mother had scooped him up and hoisted him under her arm, football style, while he thrashed his little arms and legs. A couple walked by hand in hand, skirting his flailing feet.

"They shouldn't be there."

Ronnie turned to the voice. "Gus," she said, managing to swallow the "Crazy" before it left her mouth. He scowled toward the water, his hands twisting, twisting. "What are you talking about? And where's your costume?"

"No costume tonight." He shook his head, several jerky back-and-forth movements. "No time for fun tonight. Too much danger."

"What danger, Gus?" Shadows covered his face, and Ronnie shifted so the watery rays of the setting sun could light on him. His eyes were trained on the horizon, and she glanced to where he looked before peering into his face once more. "You mean the water, the waves?"

"Not the water. Them." He pointed to the couple.

They'd moved down the beach, their shapes more shadow than anything against a sky coloring with deep oranges, purples and lilacs. Soon it would be dark. Just like in the book about the Harvest Moon Slasher.

"He doesn't like them."

Shivering at his words and the images they evoked, she asked, "'He' who?"

"Don't know his name. But I can feel him. Evil. Out there. Here." He gestured, a wide sweep of his arm that encompassed the beach to the stretch of bordering homes.

"It's just Halloween, Gus," she said, fighting a rising panic that threatened to close her throat. "We all have witches and goblins and spooks on the brain." She laughed, shutting it down before it turned manic. "Our minds play tricks on us."

Silently he stared at the couple who now appeared as dots on the darkening sand, then turned to Ronnie, his eyes clear...sane. "This is no mind trick, Miss Ronnie. It's the truth. Just ask Tom."

"Tom?"

"Matthew's grandfather, of course. He's been telling me. Evil is coming."

A gush of sympathy flowed from Ronnie's heart, and she slipped her free arm around the man's shoulders. "He's gone, Gus. It's thirty years now."

"I know that," he said, his eyes snapping as much as his voice. "But you hear him same as I do. Don't you?"

Ronnie's heart quickened, and her breath shortened so she had to force long, even draws of air. "Sometimes I like to tell myself his spirit is with us, yes. But it's my imagination. I never knew him." Before he could respond, she lifted her cooling plate. "If you'll excuse me, I'm looking for Tina. Have you seen her? I spotted her when I first came in, but it's been a while."

"Last I saw she was talking to that new fellow, the one from England. Maybe half an hour ago."

With a murmur of thanks, Ronnie turned, but Gus caught her by the arm.

"I warned her not to. There's something wrong with that one. I just can't put my finger on it."

Forcing a smile, Ronnie pulled loose from his hold and headed back toward the tables where "the Kruegers"—she really needed to learn their real last name—had been sitting. Barbara chatted with two couples from down the block, but no Fred in sight.

A tour through the house, top to bottom, had the same result—no Fred. And no Tina. She stopped by the grill where Matthew was pumping out burgers and chicken wings. "Have you seen Tina?"

He stopped, wiped his forearm along his glistening brow, and shook his head. "Not since we got here, no." He drilled his eyes into her. "Why? Something wrong?"

"No! No, nothing's wrong. I just wanted to talk to her. We're probably chasing each other in a circle."

Fighting alarm, Ronnie moved through the kitchen, then onto the second-floor deck for a view of the yard and surrounding area.

A movement below caught her attention. Two people in the shadows at the side of the house, one taller than the other, dressed in flowing black. They merged, kissed, then drew apart. Soft laughter drifted on the breeze.

"Hey, you two," Ronnie yelled, her voice light from relief, "get a room, would you?"

They looked up and Tina waved. "Just taking a break from playing host," she shouted back. "We'll be up in a few. Hold down the fort for us, will you?"

"Yeah, sure," Ronnie muttered, thinking she could have been having her own fun had she listened to her husband. But as her friends resumed their cuddling, she chuckled and turned her gaze outward.

Night had fallen, and the moon had risen halfway up the horizon, an orangey-red orb that shot streaks across the ocean's surface, making her think of trails of blood in the water...and sand.

"Fifty years ago, that might have gotten her killed."

Ronnie jerked toward the voice. Fred stood just behind to her right, another bottle of beer in his hand, thankfully without the slasher paws.

"Tina? Why?"

"A couple kissing on the beach. The dark. This is where the killings happened, isn't it?" He took a sip, his eyes focused on the couple below as if death were an everyday topic.

"The killings?" She cleared her throat. "What killings?"

"The Harvest Moon Slasher."

Nodding, wondering if he'd somehow read her mind, Ronnie said, "Yes. Thankfully after that one awful night, it never happened again." She glanced at him from the corner of her eye. "Have you read the book?"

"No, just heard about it. Is that the book you referenced earlier?"

"Yes. I have to admit, it's giving me the willies."

His eyes still trained on the beach below, he gestured toward Tina. "He chose victims like her, right, with the long, black hair?"

"That's what the book says."

"No connection was ever made between them either?"

"Other than the fact that they all committed the terrible sin of walking the beach with a lover? No."

"Sliced them right proper across the jugular, right to left from what I heard—like a leftie would—then carved a moon shape in their chests." He said it like he'd seen it firsthand. "I always wondered why he didn't kill the guys as well."

"Profilers determined it was a single male, late twenties to early thirties—"

"Who'd been wronged by a woman with long, black hair." He finished her sentence, and glanced at her, an eyebrow lifted. "Classic, no? Maybe too many beltings from his mum." He tipped the bottle, took another long swig then wiped the back of his hand across his mouth, maintaining eye contact the whole time.

"We'll never know, I guess. He disappeared. And it was half a century ago."

"So who cares anymore? Is that it?" There was an edge to his voice, an anger.

Flailing for a response, Ronnie stood rooted while his gaze traveled her face as if her opinion meant something more than it should. "I didn't say that. It seems that you do care though. Quite a bit."

He lifted his shoulders and turned his gaze back to the beach. "Just curious. I heard they had clues who the guy was, just couldn't ID him."

"That's what I read." She shot him another glance, her need to escape this strange conversation warring with her fascination with the story. "The book is based on his diary. About a week after that night, a reporter found it buried in the sand. A handwriting analysis indicated an introverted but overly critical personality, but someone very detail oriented. Investigators wondered how he could have been so sloppy."

"Or dropped purposely, a red herring to throw them off his trail."

Shivers crawled up Ronnie's spine. "What do you

mean?"

"Maybe it's all fiction. With all the clues, they never found him."

Her stomach beginning to roil, she edged toward the door. "Yeah, and if he's still alive, he's probably close to eighty years old." When he didn't respond, she said, "Listen, I can loan you the book when I'm done. That might answer some of your curiosity."

He nodded in a barely perceptible up-and-down motion of his head. "It might at that." His eyes wandered back to her face and seemed to rest on each of her features, then to the top of her head, making her want to put a scarf over her own long, black hair. "You be careful out there tonight."

"Ha ha." Another chill gripped Ronnie, and for a moment she could only stand and shake in its power. Finally she tipped her head toward the house. "Anyway, it was nice talking with you. I'm going to drag my husband away from that grill."

"He's a lucky man."

Her stomach churning, she forced a smile. "I tell him so every day," she said over her shoulder as she headed toward the cooking area.

Chapter Three

By the time Ronnie worked her way back through the crowds, Matthew had relinquished grill duty to one of the other men and was sitting at a table with a couple of guys from the neighborhood, arguing the Redskins' chance for a winning season.

She moved to his side, her anxiety calming when he slipped his arm around her waist and pulled her close. "Having fun?"

"Yeah. You?"

"No." She shrugged, uncertain how to explain her evening so far.

"What's wrong?"

"Nothing...really."

He stood and peered into her eyes. "Let's go for a

walk on the beach."

"Yes."

She clung to his hand as he led her out of the house, down the wooden steps across the dunes to the beach. The bonfire had drawn about a dozen people, and Matthew snagged her a couple marshmallows on their way past. "Here, have a snack."

"Thanks." Grinning, she sunk her teeth into the mushy white confection, and she moaned as the sugar hit her system in a rush.

"Good?"

"Mmm-hmm," she mumbled around a mouthful of sweet. When she swallowed, then licked her lips, he leaned in for a kiss.

"You taste like marshmallow," he said with a laugh a few seconds later.

"Is that a bad thing?" She looped her arms around his neck and snuggled close as a gust of chilled wind blew in, carrying the dampness of ocean air.

"Never."

A burst of laughter from the bonfire group jerked them from the moment.

"Come on," Matthew said, "let's find a spot a little less public."

One arm around her waist, he led her down the beach. After a few steps, her shoes filled with sand, and she paused to toe them off, then bent to pick them up.

"Let me," Matthew said as he plucked them from the ground. "You always did prefer your toes in the sand." His voice teased and flirted, even with such an innocuous statement, making her insides go squishy.

They walked like that, cuddling, without talking, until the party's lights and laughter faded. Until the sounds and scents of the beach at night closed around them. Waves at low tide shushed fifty feet to their left. Somewhere to their right a creature flapped its wings. And far off, came the long, lonely blast of a ship's horn.

"Hey." Matthew's voice, soft and questioning, drew her from her musings. She looked up and caught his gaze as he turned her into his arms. "I love you," he said as his mouth covered hers. His arms held her close and secure, like she was precious to him. Breathless, they broke apart, and he skimmed his lips along her shoulder, making her shiver with something more than the chilled air. She tucked her face into the nest between his chin and shoulder, tasting salt and sand, and burrowed closer, wanting to mesh herself to his body.

As though reading her thoughts, he molded his hands along her hips and behind, then groaned and said, half laughing, "There's something about this dress that's driving me crazy. It's so...prim."

"Oh, is it? And you like prim?"

"I do tonight." He groaned again. "We've made an appearance. Tina's in good hands. I think we should ditch the party and go home."

"I like the way you think." Her breathing shallow, something liquid-y and hot running through her veins, she stepped back and bent to put her shoes on. As her fingers grasped the heels, a nearby animal growled, low and menacing.

She straightened with a gasp and squinted into the dark. A structure squatted on stilts just over the nearest dune. The old beach cottage, Fred's childhood home. She'd forgotten it was here, near the end of this section of beach that curved away from the roadway.

A wide porch led to a short lawn of beach scrabble that swept toward the water but stopped at a four-foot seawall protecting the house from damaging tides. At the edge of the wall, a cat crouched, its golden eyes narrowed and focused on the row of dunes. It growled again, its fur standing to attention as if stroked with an electric wand. Ronnie followed its gaze, searching for the unknown. With a final shriek, it launched itself toward the house and scampered under the stilts, to the far corner of the property, where it cowered, eyes glowing yellow in the black.

Apparently unaware, Matthew took her hand and drew her forward, away from whatever it was that felt dark and threatening. Fighting the urge to turn and watch for trailing danger, she told herself it was only her imagination on high alert. There was no one on the beach but the two of them. Still, she hurried her steps and stumbled, hoping Matthew would think it was ardor that had caused her clumsiness. Even his strong, sure embrace couldn't stop the tremors that nearly rooted her feet in the sand.

"Cold?" He dropped her hand, moved his arm to her shoulders.

"No, just...." She turned her head to peek, hoping he wouldn't notice. He did. He stopped and peered into the night, first forward, then to their rear. The little house looked only feet away, like they'd been going backward instead of forward.

"Anyone there?" he shouted, the breeze stealing his voice as it left his throat.

Still quaking from the unseen and probably imagined evil, she grabbed for his hand. "No one, honey. I've just got the creeps. Let's go."

He stood unmoving while she tugged on his hand, then finally turned and joined her. "It's that damn book, isn't it? It's got you imagining all sorts of things."

She nodded, telling herself it was the truth. "It is Halloween. And the Slasher killed his victims along this stretch of beach. That Fred guy got me thinking, again.

He seemed oddly interested in a story that's fifty years old."

"Don't worry about him. George and I are keeping an eye on him."

"Why?" She leaned back to look into his face, but he'd closed off his expression.

"Anyone who says he has no secrets—it's just a feeling that he's not what he says he is."

"You think he's dangerous?"

"No. I don't get those vibes. But something's off. Stop worrying, would you? Try putting that vivid imagination to good use, like what we'll do when we get home."

He dipped his head and nibbled at her ear. Ronnie laughed at the sensation, but couldn't help another glance behind.

As she turned back, a whiff of something woodsy and spicy tickled her nose, reminding her of the cologne Matthew had dug from the attic, and what felt like a million shocks erupted beneath her skin. She whipped around.

Behind them, a couple danced along the seawall at Fred's cottage. The ocean breeze blew the woman's hair—long, loose and black—straight behind her, like a flag. She wore a cocktail dress, something light and airy with a top layer of netting that caught the moon's reddish glow. The man wore a black dinner jacket with a skinny black tie and skinny black pants. They weren't so much dancing as swaying in place, his arms around her waist, hers around his neck, and they held each other's gaze.

They were familiar to her, but she couldn't place them. Maybe a couple of party-goers who'd had a bit too much of the spiked punch had wandered this far down the beach.

Still, the movements were stilted and stiff, not loose-limbed, as a drunk's would be. And he apparently had doused himself with an entire bottle of the cologne. As she and Matthew neared, the aroma grew and grew until it burned the pathway from Ronnie's nose to her throat. Until every breath singed her lungs as if she'd swallowed a fireball. "Don't you smell that?"

He stopped short, sighed and gave her a look that told her he was losing patience. "I don't smell a damn thing."

"It must be that man."

"What man?"

She jerked her head toward the couple on the wall. "The guy on the wall, dancing with the woman."

Matt squinted, his gaze following where she pointed. "There's no one there, Ron."

"What?" Ronnie blinked and focused. They were...

gone. "I swear, there was a man and woman on top of the wall, dancing."

He stared at her face for a long moment, his eyes questioning. "I'm throwing that book out when we get home. Come on." He took her hand in a firm grip, as if he were afraid to let go, and trudged forward.

She would have rebuked him, but she was beginning to question her own sanity. Still, her shoulders wouldn't stop twitching, and she snuck another glance behind. Nothing there but the ocean, the empty beach and a big orange ball in the sky shedding a path of rust-colored moonlight in the sand.

A breeze gusted parallel to the shore, pushing them along, as if Mother Nature sensed her husband's urgency to get home and wanted to help.

As she tried to calm her galloping heart, a shadow darted past in her peripheral vision. A man, tall—well over six feet. A hoodie shadowed his face, giving him a ghoulish appearance. She squeaked, tried to point, but Matthew yanked on her hand, pulling her sideways. Then he dropped like a bowling ball at her feet.

Had she had any air in her lungs, she would have screamed, but she could only muster a croak as the man lifted his arm—his left arm—over his head like he wanted to bash her skull in. Now she screamed. She pivoted, her bare feet twisting in the cool sand. But the man was too quick and too big. He clamped his right hand over her mouth and pinched her nose until black dots swam in front of her eyes.

"I've got you now," he grunted into her left ear. Her mind froze. The accent. Fred's. "And this time you'll stay buried."

Chapter Four

Awareness eventually came, first with the sensation of grit in her mouth, sand crunching between her molars and making her gag.

A hard dampness beneath her, against her back.

Next, a rhythmic roar and rumbling that could only be the sea.

Then smell. Dank, rotting wood. Salt, the kind from the sea, with a kicker of dead fish.

She remembered then—the man with the knife. Fred? He'd attacked Matthew, left him unconscious in the sand. Or dead.

Retching, she rolled onto her side. When the sensation passed, she focused on her last memory. Whoever had attacked—and her money was on Fred what's-his-name—hadn't killed her. Yet. He'd brought her here. Wherever "here" was. She could still hope.

She opened her eyes—seeing nothing but black—and eased into a supine position to take stock. First she lifted her legs, one at a time, then wiggled her toes. All working. No pain. She stretched her arms as high as she could above her, rocking from side to side to reach her limit. Then she switched, extending them to either side, again stretching. No restrictions on her movement, no walls closing her in, at least within the distance of her arms' reach. Wherever she was, it wasn't a coffin.

For a moment she had to close her eyes against a wave of relieved dizziness, but she pried them open. As they began to adjust to the dark, boxy shapes took form to her right, stacked two or three high, about a dozen altogether. A storage area?

Forcing herself to focus through the sound of her heart pounding in her ears, she sat up, then moved to her knees and began searching with her hands, fingers splayed, palms down. Starting close to her body, she worked out in concentric arcs, first the air, then the floor.

It was cement-like, rock hard and rough beneath her palms and knees. After a few swipes, her hand ran into something, both solid but pliable, like leather. Another tentative reach and she wrapped her hand around it—a shoe. Her shoe. After a few more reaches, she found the other one.

Deciding not to analyze what that meant—that he'd found her shoes and tossed them in here with her...hiding any evidence of her existence—she put them aside, shifted and crawled a few feet forward.

Something crunched beneath her knee.

Squelching a scream, she maneuvered backward and forced herself to look at what she'd been kneeling on. Tiny light-colored fragments rested in a line. A few inches beyond, a longer section about three inches long. Bones? From an animal?

Fascinated despite the fear that had a chokehold on her ribcage, she began to pat the ground surrounding the fragments. A few inches west of the line, her fingers landed on something stiff but pliable. Not bone. Cloth? Petrified from years of exposure? A burial cloth for a beloved pet?

She stopped herself from smacking her head at the ridiculous thought. The man—Fred?—had said something about *staying* buried, then dumped her here with—

The reality of what that meant hit with furnace-like heat, followed by an icy wash of fear. She dropped her head into her lap and breathed through the terror.

Calmer, and determined to get herself out of this,

whatever this was, she lifted her torso and reached again for the material. It was trapped, so she tugged, then tugged harder, and harder, and in a space of thirty seconds had freed a foot-long section. It felt grainy between her fingers, like a fine netting.

She rose to her knees for leverage and yanked. A box to her left toppled, and a wad of fabric came free. She spread it out and felt along its edges. It formed a circle, made of netting and satin. A skirt. Above it, a rectangular segment in satin with skinny straps on either side—a bodice. It was a cocktail dress, much like the one worn by the woman dancing on the seawall. Presumably last worn by the skeleton sharing her space.

Shudders shimmied from Ronnie's neck to her feet, and she had to brace her hands on the floor while the tremors gripped her. When they passed, she wiped a row of sweat from her upper lip, then sat back on her heels to think. To plan her way out of this hellhole.

There had to be a way out, after all. Fred hadn't transported her here by scrambling her atoms and shooting them through space and time. He'd had to carry her here.

She shifted her weight again, this time to the balls of her feet, then stood, slowly, her arms making slow sweeps ahead and above her in the near black. When she stood erect, meeting no resistance, she slid a foot forward, then another, counting so she could retrace her steps to her origin.

On the tenth step, her shin knocked into something hard, making her cringe. She leaned over to rub the offended leg, then focused her gaze on the spot where she'd hit. A vague outline, flat and long. Another one several inches above, but forward. Another beyond that.

A stairway. A way out.

Sobs gathered in her belly and threatened to overflow, but she forced them back with giant breaths that expanded and contracted her entire midsection. Then, using her hands as guides, climbed.

She counted to seven when her head whacked something hard. An overhead door? Balancing on one knee, she reached up and pushed against the obstruction. No give. She pushed harder and took a step up to put her shoulder into the effort, groaning as she fought for leverage. Failing, she descended a few steps and started to pound on the door while she screamed for help.

She kept it up until she was hoarse, until the heels of her hands were raw and her legs trembled from the stress of holding her position.

Whimpering, she turned and sat on a step to indulge in a moment of self-pity before looking for an alternate escape. She gave herself to the count of thirty, doggedly refusing to allow her mind to track to the image of her husband, to think about whether he was hurt, or dead, when a metallic *thunk* from overhead nearly tumbled her from her perch.

The door swung open, flooding her prison with moonlight. She twisted to face the opening, then lifted a hand over her eyes to shield them from the sudden brightness. Still, she could barely open them, could barely make out the wizened face peering into the opening.

"Gus? How—"

"No time, Miss Ronnie. Come."

He extended a hand through the opening. She clasped it, its warmth spreading from her palm to her toes, then took a step up. She made it halfway out and had braced her palms against the frame to take the last few steps to freedom, when a man appeared, race-walking in a lumbering gait down a nearby dune. As he neared, Ronnie got a glimpse of leathery skin, black eyes, and a feathering of white hair under a black brimmed cap with the blue-and-white cross of Scotland on the front.

Behind him, the old beach cottage skulked in the dark, hiding its secrets.

"Damn you, Gus. You don't belong here. You're ruining everything." His voice rasped and was garbled with age and exertion, but the accent...Fred's.

Gus rose stiffly to his feet, then twisted to face him. When the old man swung, Gus ducked, but he was too slow. He staggered, but held his ground. "Run, Miss Ronnie. Run!"

And oh how she wanted to run, but the sight of Crazy Gus grappling with this person, fighting for his life, and hers, held her in place. Then Gus spoke, and she was transfixed.

"I knew it was you all these years, Angus, you evil bastard. You took my Annie. I tried to tell them, but they wouldn't listen. She's down there, isn't she?'"

Gus lunged, head down, and tackled the other man—Angus—in the midsection. The two rolled on the ground, throwing punches that seemed to have no effect on the other.

Angus ended up on top and straddled Gus, his hands around his throat. "She was mine first. You stole her. I couldn't let you just take her. Don't you see?"

Distracted, he didn't notice Ronnie's approach. She grabbed him around the shoulders and hung on, drawing his attention long enough for Gus to pry the man's hands from around his throat. "She left you because you were an abusive bastard. She told me everything. You left that fake note in my house to make everyone believe she'd run back to you. But I knew better. And all this time she's been dead, and nearly in my backyard. I couldn't stop you then, but by God I'll stop you now."

Roaring, Angus reared back, tossing Ronnie off his back like a ragdoll. She landed flat-footed, and shooting pains stabbed into her calf as she righted herself and prepared to run.

The two men stood in a swath of orange moonlight, swinging at each other like brawling drunks. Then, as if he'd only been playing, Angus reared back and backhanded Gus with such force, the old man's head snapped to the side, and his body crumpled to the ground, landing silently in a sprawl.

The killer spun toward Ronnie, anger thrumming in his voice, hate filling his eyes. "She would be at rest if not for you. Now her filthy, broken life is revealed to the world. She would hate that. I hate that." He reached into his jacket and withdrew a knife that looked like it could gut a bear. The blade shone red in the moon's reflection. "I didn't plan on doing this. You've left me no choice."

Trancelike, as if seeing herself from a distance, Ronnie edged in the direction of the roadway a couple hundred yards to her rear, trying to hide the cramping in her leg. Still she couldn't help questioning. "What others? Why'd you kill Annie? Because her life was broken, dirty?"

The man grunted but kept moving, his hands gripping and regripping the knife's handle. "She was mine. We went to university together. We planned to marry. Then she betrayed me. She broke it off. Started seeing other men, like him." He jerked his head toward Crazy Gus, who lay motionless. His voice held a tremor that hadn't been there before. He'd been hurt, in his own sick, twisted way.

Ronnie glanced to her rear while she backpedaled, one slow step at a time. "Then she married him. Is that why you killed her?"

He snorted, a prideful sound. "For her betrayal, yes."

"And what about the others? They hadn't hurt you."

"Ah, but they had. So like her, parading around the beach, every one of them, showing off their filthy relationships with those boys, as if they were real men." A smile grew on his lips, and he looked down at his hands, then turned them so his palms were open, the knife resting flat. In her head, Ronnie saw it, and his hands, dripping blood. "They deserved to die. She deserved to die."

Somehow Ronnie sensed his gathering strength, and as she turned to run, another scream whipping up her throat, he lunged, knife in his hand. But her leg collapsed beneath her, and she fell, landing with a thud on her back in the sand. Instantly he was on top, pinning her down with a hand around her throat and the other overhead, holding the knife in a kill grip. Behind him, the moon pulsed with its red-orange glow as if mocking her stupidity. She should have run. Now it was too late.

Struggling for breath, she braced against his knife arm with one hand while she clawed at his hand around her neck. But he outweighed her, outreached her, and even at his age, overpowered her. She rolled and thrashed, tried to buck herself free, only making him laugh and wheeze.

He leaned in with his foul-smelling breath. "You shouldn't have intruded. This is your fault."

His hold on her neck intensified, and her legs twitched as she struggled to focus, to stay alert. She was gagging, coughing, when that smell, that spicy/woodsy smell, rolled over them in a dense fog.

Her attacker shook his head like a dog who'd stuck his nose in pepper.

The scent intensified, and behind him, the dancing couple appeared—just materialized—on the sea wall. She stilled, her eyes fixed on the apparition, and Angus snapped his head around to follow her gaze. "Leave me alone, dammit. Stop tormenting me."

The couple continued their swaying, oblivious

to what was going on twenty feet below them on the beach. The smell grew to a stench, then got worse.

Growling, Angus turned back to Ronnie and lifted the knife overhead in a double-handed grip.

"Da, stop!" Fred's voice, carried by the sea breeze, pierced Ronnie's daze. As she thrust her hands up to stop the knife's plunge, the man's weight lifted in one swoop.

Choking, tears streaming down her face, she clamored to her feet, feeling thick, like a drunk. Fred held the old man from behind, an arm around his throat, his opposite hand on the older man's wrist. He squeezed the wrist, his face contorting with effort, and the knife fell. Fred kicked it, and it sailed across the sand, landing point down, a foot away from her.

A siren wailed from somewhere close by, and Fred jerked his head toward the road. "Go. You're safe now. I've got him. I've finally got him."

Chapter Five

Several hours later, Ronnie sat in an interview room at the local police station, trying to make sense of all that had happened since leaving for the party that afternoon. Matthew held her hand like he'd never let go. Crazy Gus sat on the other side of the small conference table, recovered from his earlier knock-out, and Fred... whoever...sat sad-faced across from them.

Matthew had met her as she stumbled through the cottage's yard, the grass cold and wet but feeling so alive beneath her bare feet. He'd grabbed her, hauled her close so her breath expelled in a whoosh, and her nose crushed into the soft folds of his grandfather's sweater. Her teeth chattering, she tried to talk, but he shushed her.

"Just let me hold you a minute." He'd been shaking too—his arms, his voice. "I came to and you were gone. George and I searched. You weren't home. You weren't at Tina's. You weren't anywhere. Then Fred found us and told us his suspicions. I nearly died a thousand deaths when I realized the killer—the damn killer from the book—had you, fifty years later."

He pulled her tighter. "Are you okay? Tell me you're okay."

"I'm okay. Are you? Let me see your head. You probably have a concussion."

"And you're limping."

They stood, clutching each other, until a cop walked by, tossed a blanket in their direction, then told them to wait in a cruiser. Finally easing back, Matthew draped the blanket around her shoulders. "We'll get checked out tomorrow, but we need to make statements. Let's get this over with."

His voice was tight, his hold tighter as they walked toward the waiting police car, its siren silent but its lights still flashing the blue-and-red of danger.

At the station, after giving her statement to a detective, she was shown to a separate room where the others waited. As she sat, Fred leaned forward. "I'm so very sorry for what my father put you through."

She nodded, then cleared her throat. "So, he really

is the...the Slasher?"

Fred held up a hand. "I'll answer all your questions. But I also need to apologize for misleading you."

She glanced to Matt, whose one eyebrow had quirked in that told-you-so expression.

"He's not in 'securities,' like he told us."

Fred reached into his jacket pocket and withdrew a black leather case, then flipped it open to reveal a star-like badge with a crown at the top. "Metropolitan Police, London."

"Scotland Yard?"

He gave a thin-lipped smile as he flipped the case closed and slipped it back into his pocket. "That's right."

"So you moved to the States..."

"I moved here, both times, to track down my father." His mouth twisted with the last word, as if he'd eaten something rotten. He caught her gaze. "My ma, his wife, was his last victim."

Ronnie's eyes moistened. "I'm sorry, but—"

"But you still have many questions." When she nodded, he continued. "They were living here—that part was true. I am U.S. born. He and Mr. Johnson," he pointed at Gus, "had been friends with your husband's grandfather, at university."

Ronnie glanced to Matt. He didn't look surprised.

"They all fell in love with the same girl. Annie. My grandfather dated her, and so did Fred's father, but she dumped them both for Gus." Matthew smiled, a slow lift of his lips that acknowledged the older man's victory.

"That's right, she did." Gus's voice drifted off with his gaze.

Something frizzled in Ronnie's brain. "The girl in the photo. Your grandfather is dancing with a young woman with long black hair."

"That was them, Annie and Tom," Gus said, nodding. "They had some laughs, but Tom found his true love." He tipped his chin toward Matthew. "Your grandmother."

"And Annie found hers." Ronnie took the old man's hand in hers. It shook, but he gave hers a squeeze before letting go.

"Yes, she did. We married, planned a family. It was Angus McGowan, Fred's father, who couldn't forget. He never went back to England, instead moved to somewhere out in the Midwest, married a woman that looked like my Annie."

"My mother," Fred said, picking up the story. "I like to think they were happy for a time. They had me. There had to be some love there."

"Whatever is was, it wasn't enough." Gus's voice

sliced into Fred's musings, cutting him off.

"We moved here when I was five. Da was always angry, always yelling. And he'd disappear for nights at a stretch. Ma put up a good front, but she was miserable."

"The bastard was stalking my wife. When she had nothing to do with him, he went nuts." Gus circled his ear with his finger.

"And that's when the killings happened." Ronnie looked from one to the other, trying to follow the story's thread.

"Must have been." Gus nodded, his folded hands twisting together. "He must have taken her first, stashed her in that hidden cellar in his house, but when he killed the others, he left them on the beach." He glanced to Fred. "Rotten son-of-a-bitch even left his own wife there like a piece of trash."

Fred flinched but held the old man's gaze. "He did at that. Do you think I'll ever forget the sight of my ma dead on the beach? Her murder was chalked up to the Harvest Moon Slasher, and if the cops even looked at Da, nothing stuck. He disappeared, just like the book says, and my aunt came, took me to the U.K."

Gus cleared his throat and wiped a line of moisture from beneath his eyes. "When your mother was killed, the cops searched your house but never found a thing.

Never knew that cellar was there."

"Neither did I. Not until tonight."

Ronnie narrowed her eyes at Fred. "It really is your childhood home?"

He nodded. "I came back to the States on a football scholarship, like I told you, started digging around in the history of that night."

When he paused, his gaze staring into the past, Ronnie said, "So when you moved here recently, you must have had some inkling..." She couldn't bring herself to say more. There was enough anguish in the man's eyes already.

"Right. When I moved back home after university, my aunt confided in me. Said my ma had told her of Da's temper, his beatings." Fred's voice cracked, and he took a breath before continuing. "He'd been a nasty child, and she'd always suspected him of killing Ma. Which would have made odds that he was the Slasher.

"So I made it my mission to find the bastard and dig out the truth. If it was him, I swore to make him pay for what he'd done to those women, to me, and to Ma. I got hired on by MPS, specialized in profiling. It gave me resources."

The detective in charge of the case knocked on the door. "You can go now, all of you. Officers will drive you home." He gestured toward Fred. "Inspector

McGowan, your father is being held on suspicion of murder. If you'd like to speak to him—"

"I wouldn't."

"All right. We'll be in touch."

The four of them looked at each other, but remained seated, seemingly reluctant to break up.

"What I don't understand," Ronnie said, nodding toward Gus, "was how you knew where to find me."

"It was Tom and Annie. They pointed the way." He said it matter-of-factly, as if the thought of communing with two dead people wasn't the slightest out of the ordinary.

"Wait a minute." Matthew said half laughing. "What are you talking about?"

"The two of them, dancing together on the top of the seawall. Didn't you see them when you walked by?" The pitch in Gus's voice rose. "And you had to smell it, didn't you? Your grandfather's cologne? The stuff stank to high heaven, even back in college."

Matthew, eyes blinking and mouth gaping, turned to Ronnie. "Uh, no. No, I didn't, but it seems my wife did."

Ronnie could only give him her own told-you-so smile.

"Yeah, she and I are simpatico like that, aren't we, Miss Ronnie?"

"That we are."

An officer stopped in the doorway. "Mr. Johnson, I can take you home now."

Gus pushed to his feet, his joints popping, and Ronnie stood, ignoring the twinge in her calf, to give him a hug. "Thank you. Please let me know if you need any help with arrangements for Annie, or anything."

The body hidden in the old cellar was removed for examination and identification, but Gus had recognized the clothes as his wife's, and no one doubted that it was her.

Gus sniffled. "I might take you up on it. Want to do it proper. She'll be watching from heaven, you know."

Ronnie drew in a huge breath to fight back tears as the old man followed the officer out.

As they left the station minutes later, Matthew shook Fred's hand. "One final question for you. How did you know your father would show up here? Why now? And how did you happen to find them at the house just in time to save my wife? Were you communicating with my dead grandfather as well?"

Fred leaned against the wall, his arms crossed over his chest, and stared at his feet before meeting Matt's gaze. "It was a gamble. I suspected the book, publishing his diary, would draw him out. Tonight is the fiftieth anniversary."

"Wait a minute." Ronnie studied his face. "You wrote the book?"

"I did. Under a pseudonym."

"So the diary wasn't found by a reporter?"

"No, it was found by my aunt, who gave it to me and told me to get the son-of-a-bitch who'd killed my ma."

"Huh. Imagine that."

They headed to the parking lot where officers waited to give them rides. Ronnie and Matthew moved to one of the cruisers, and as Matthew held her door for her, she shouted to Fred, "Let me know when you release the sequel."

A few minutes later, they pulled into their driveway just as the sun began its climb up the horizon, casting a path of lavender and gold across the water.

After a quick shower, Ronnie hobbled to bed and snuggled into her husband's waiting arms.

"Matt?"

"Hmm?" His voice was thick with encroaching sleep.

"Let's stay in next Halloween."

Epilogue

I lie in this prison cell, covered with a rough blanket that carries the odor of those who came before me—and hope for the oblivion of death. My days are numbered, whether by nature or law, but I'm ready. I've seen the future.

He stood before me, tall and proud and righteous, looking so much like his mother—her with her pious anger—that for a moment, rage squirmed like ants beneath my skin. Then I saw beneath his contempt to the man—my son, who is half me. And I rejoiced. My death is not an end but a beginning.

Blood always tells.

"Freddy? Fred?" Barbara moved into Fred's office, lathering her hands with the skin cream she used every night. She said it hid the wrinkles. It didn't. "Come to bed, sugar. It's been a long, awful night."

"That it has. Be right up, love."

Fred saved the file and took a quick look before closing the laptop. The new story was shaping up well.

Three, After Midnight

by

Alexa Day

Dedication

For every woman who has ever sized up that hot stranger at the bar.

H alloween had begun three full minutes ago. And while Deirdre knew she should wake the man next to her so that she could get started, she hesitated.

This one was so different. It might not even work this time.

The others had reminded her of her husband, at least on the surface. Tall and lean, with softer voices and long, angular features. An engineer, an account manager, an executive trainer, all strictly white-collar types.

Not this one.

Tonight she shared her bed with a wrestling coach, whose muscular, winter-tanned body lay facedown on the pillows next to her. The broad back that rose and fell beneath her sheets had stretched a hunter green hoodie to its limits. His thick fingers had caught her eye as he fidgeted with the label on a bottle of PBR at her traditional Halloween dive bar. He taught French at Bowman High, called himself Trip, and had thighs that felt like iron beneath his worn jeans.

She'd put her hand on his leg after just two drinks and smiled when the muscle went taut beneath her palm. She'd surprised him. Her forwardness had shocked her, too; she typically needed another drink before making her move. But she didn't have time to waste this year. Trip was different, and she'd need time to try again with someone else if it ended up being weird this time.

Weird for whom?

She could hardly argue that it would be strange for her, now that she'd enjoyed the wrestling coach so thoroughly. Her limbs ached as she rolled onto her side, away from the clock and toward his sleeping form. He'd fulfilled all the promises his body had made. An athlete's stamina and the sort of physique that inspired fantasies and works of art. Still, he'd been gentle with her on the whole. He'd loved her like a stranger who hoped to see her again, or at least one who hoped to be remembered fondly in girls' night gossip.

Trip was not so different from the others in practice, really, but in his potential. He definitely had the tools. Cam would happily supply everything else.

That'll be a change for him, won't it? She had to bite her lip to keep from giggling at the thought of her husband's response.

Trip, for all his open-mindedness, would probably think it was weird, too.

He doesn't get a vote.

She caressed his arm, her hand riding up over the warm contours of his biceps to the ridge of his shoulder blade. Her thumb teased his earlobe before she pushed all that sand-colored hair out of her way. When none of that woke him, she pressed her body along the length of his and touched her tongue to the baby-soft skin where his sideburn ended.

He came to life slowly. "Mmm. Hey." Sleep had added a sandpaper edge to his deep voice.

"Happy Halloween," she whispered.

He opened his slate gray eyes and offered her a devilish grin. "Happy Halloween to you, too." He pushed himself up and over onto one elbow to face her. "Is this a trick or a treat?"

She wrapped one leg around the thigh that had tempted her earlier that evening. "What do you think?"

"Feels like a treat." He covered her body with his, angling himself over her, and she pressed her hands to the back of his neck, pulling him down to her until his full, generous mouth met her lips.

What time is it?

She tugged at his hair until he pushed himself away from her. The man kissed like a castaway at a banquet, and he tasted so very good, but she didn't have time to be distracted.

"What's wrong?" Real concern showed on his face.

"Nothing." She propped herself up on her elbows. "I just needed a favor."

He kissed her again, his tongue teasing the delicate flesh just inside her mouth before he withdrew. "Anything for you," he whispered. In the soft openness of his voice, she heard more of the gentle kindness that came through in his lovemaking. When he said "anything," he meant it.

Maybe this wouldn't be so strange after all.

"I need some ice," she said. Her chest burned with longing to squeeze his thigh between hers one last time. "Would you go downstairs and get me a glass of ice?"

"You need ice?" That wicked grin reappeared on his face. Did he know what the ice was for? He really was different.

She nodded. "Just a glass of ice. The fridge has an icemaker on the door. I like it crushed."

The grin broadened into a smile. He did know what it was for.

"You got it," he said. He rose from bed, his thick erection bobbing as he left the room.

She'd dared to hope for a man like this—kind, open-minded, and a tireless sexual dynamo—and now that he was here in the flesh, she really hoped this wouldn't end up being weird.

The stairs creaked beneath his weight. She pressed her tongue to the roof of her mouth and strained to hear him. A man like Trip, who knew how to use his body to control the bodies of others, would move gracefully all the time and quietly when he had to. She didn't expect to hear anything more, unless he got all the way to the icemaker.

Cam would probably stop him before then.

The silence stretched on downstairs. She glanced at the clock again: 12:45.

Come on.

A soft thump, like something heavy being jostled on the living room rug, made her sit up in bed. She craned her neck toward the door. Had Trip bumped into the armchair in the dark?

Or had it started?

Another thump answered her question. That chair was in an awkward place, but no one bumped into it twice.

Something scraped the hardwood floor down

there, followed by a crash that made the walls shudder, a strangled cry forced through clenched teeth. It had never gone on like this before. She rubbed her sticky palms against the sheets. What if it didn't work? What if Trip came back up here and—

Then, as suddenly as it had begun, the noise stopped. She strained toward the doorway, as if something inside her could reach out for the sound.

A familiar whirring broke the silence, followed by loud clinking. The icemaker.

She dropped back onto the bed with a sigh and waited to hear her husband's heavy gait on the stairs. It had worked. Cam might still decide it was weird, but she wouldn't mind convincing him that a little weirdness would be worth it.

"This is *nice*." Trip's voice filled the hallway, but the coach's easy-going West Coast drawl had been replaced by Cam's brisk inflection. "*Very* nice."

Relief mingled with joy, and her vision blurred. She swallowed and swiped at her eyes as her husband entered their bedroom with the glass of crushed ice. He paused just inside the doorway and stretched his free arm in front of him.

Well, Trip's free arm. His *borrowed* arm, attached to the rest of his borrowed body.

Cam walked around in a circle, trying to get used

to Trip's beautifully built form.

"You like it?" she asked.

"Hell, yeah," Cam said. "Yeah."

He went to the dresser and set the glass down on the corner, where his morning and evening habits had formed a water stain after years of dodging coasters, napkins, and other forms of protection. He stood before the mirror, admiring the unfamiliar body, running big hands over powerful arms, just as she had. Cam pushed his hand through Trip's hair and then mussed it roughly.

"He needs a haircut," she said.

Cam regarded her reflection with a mischievous glimmer in his eye. "Should we do that for him?"

She laughed. "That's not very sporting."

"No. I guess it's not." He smoothed his palms over his chest and down over his legs before taking his cock in his hand. "God, he's big."

She'd watched Cam stand in front of that mirror so many mornings, struggling with a tie or his short, wiry hair, ignoring her constant complaints about the water stain on the dresser. She didn't think she'd taken him for granted; she hadn't had time. But she hadn't stopped to say how much she loved the sight of him, even doing those everyday things. She hadn't found the words, the way to say it without drifting into something maudlin and unnecessary.

And then she'd lost her chance.

She got out of bed and wrapped her arms around him, resting her head in the space between his shoulders, where the column of his neck began. She closed her eyes, and for a moment, she could feel the bony ridge of Cam's spine beneath her cheek instead of Trip's brawny frame.

"Cameron?"

"Yeah, babe?"

The rumble of his voice against her breasts made her pull him closer. "Is this weird?" she asked.

He chuckled. "A little." She opened her eyes as he turned around to face her. "Okay, let's just be straight with each other. This guy is a lot better looking than I was."

She couldn't help but laugh at his expression, the raised eyebrow that urged her to fess up. "I wouldn't say that…"

"Come on. *You're* not dead." He touched his forehead to hers.

"I mean, he's bigger than you are. Were. Sure." She moved even closer to him, until his hard-on pressed against her belly. "I just didn't want it to be weird. He's so different."

"Is he?" he whispered. The heat of Trip's voice, combined with Cam's suggestive intent, made something unravel inside her. "How's he so different?"

She slid her palm along the smooth skin of his erection. "He's a wrestling coach. So he knows how to move." She made a fist around his shaft and squeezed. "Like a dancer."

"Mmm. Wrestling coach." He sighed. "That explains a lot of things." He pushed his hips toward her, and she smoothed her thumb over the head of his cock. "What else?"

"Well. He's so…gentle. I mean, everyone's been *gentle*, but this one is really sweet."

"Oh, yeah?" He kissed the top of her head, and she breathed in the spicy-sweet scent of this borrowed body. "Maybe we can teach him a thing or two."

Her skin prickled and grew warm. "I think he knows what the ice is for."

"Really?" He toyed with her hair, stroked her collarbone all the way to her shoulder. "That *would* be different."

His hands cupped her face, and she kissed him, opening herself to him for what felt like the first time and the last time. He explored her body with long, slow caresses, and she wondered if they'd be able to spend the rest of the night like this, just kissing each other with the dresser at his back. As wonder turned to hope, he pulled away and whispered, "The ice is melting."

She giggled. "I guess we'd better hurry, then."

She reached past him to the glass, where the ice had begun to form a slush. She felt his gaze on her like a spotlight, warming her skin as she let some of the half-melted slurry slide into her mouth. She replaced the glass in its circle of water.

He leaned back against the dresser and held her hands as she lowered herself to her knees before him. Carefully, holding the remnants of slush on her tongue, she parted her lips just enough to admit the tip of his cock. He sucked in a breath above her and then let it out on a groan.

"Oh, my God," he whispered. "Oh, holy God."

She took him slowly, inch by inch, mindful of the rapidly melting ice and the sheer size of him. She closed her lips tight around his thick shaft. The last of the slush melted against his heated flesh, and she swirled the cool water around him with her tongue, sucking greedily at him. He gasped and whispered her name. When she plunged toward him, his broad hand settled on top of her head.

She slid her tongue up and down the underside of his cock, matching the rhythm of his hips and taking him as deeply as she could. Her body responded to his every groan and sigh, and her arousal surged alongside his until he lifted his hand.

The broken contact made her look up at him. Something other than pleasure contorted his face now. His eyes were squeezed shut, and his brows drew together in a grimace.

"He's really strong." Cam spoke through clenched teeth.

She released his cock and wiped water from her lips with the back of her hand. "What?"

"He's fighting me." Trip's formidable muscles went taut, and he shook his head fiercely, as if trying to avoid a horde of insects. "He's fighting to get back."

She sat back on her haunches and then edged away from him. "He's what?"

Cam groaned, and she recognized the strangled sound she'd heard from downstairs. "I'm sorry, babe. I can't—"

She reached upward for the bed, missed, and landed hard on her ass. Before her, her man fought to stay in another man's body.

And he was losing.

Trip's body bucked against the dresser, knocking the glass from its precarious perch onto the carpeted floor. She shuddered as she watched his body lashing out at itself, twisting and lurching as it tried to shake off the psychic intrusion. She scrambled onto the bed. Her skin erupted in goosebumps, and she tugged at the rumpled sheets.

She'd put this into motion. She'd chosen this man, so much stronger and more self-aware than the others. She'd done this. And now, somehow, she had to stop this.

She reached blindly for the nightstand, hoping that one of the things she looked at every night had transformed into something she could use as a weapon. Her hand closed around the neck of her bedside lamp, and the plug came free of the outlet when she tugged at it, upsetting the picture frames and candle holders that surrounded it. The lampshade wobbled from its perch and dropped to the floor as the man in her bedroom stopped struggling. Panting, he bent at the waist, his hands on his knees.

Her grip on the lamp loosened, and she watched him catch his breath.

"Cam?" she whispered.

His eyes met hers, and defeat swelled and sank in her chest.

"What the fuck just happened in here?" asked Trip. His voice made a harsh echo against the bedroom walls.

Her hand trembled on the lamp. He took a half-step toward the door, pausing with his hoodie beneath one foot. Trip was poised to defend himself, to lunge at her or spring away, as a wrestling coach would be. She just wasn't sure if the fight was over. Had he purged Cam completely?

"Trip?" she asked.

"Yeah! What happened?"

"Shit," she whispered. She lifted her free hand in a defensive gesture of her own. "It's hard to explain."

Where is he?

Trip bent his knees. "Explain, hell. Put that down."

Instinct made her grip the lamp harder. Cam was supposed to get back in, take control, protect her. Where was he?

Trip was moving toward her now, one slow half-step, then another. "I don't want to hurt you, honey, but you've got to put that down."

"We don't want to hurt you, either," she said. "Just stop for a second and listen."

"We?" He advanced another half-step, staring at the lamp in her hand.

"I know how this must sound. But we didn't hurt you. Nobody hurt you."

He nodded briskly, and then, moving so quickly she could hardly see him, he seized her free hand and yanked her into an embrace. His arms locked her against his hard, sweat-slick chest, her back and hips trapped against his hot skin. The lamp spun harmlessly away to the floor.

"Let go." She tried to struggle, for his sake rather than hers. "I don't want him to hurt you."

"Dammit, who are you talking about?"

Why hadn't he taken over yet? Had Trip somehow hurt him? "My husband."

"Is he in here?"

The bedroom door slammed with a startling crack, hard enough to make her ears ring. A long sigh of relief slipped from her, and she stopped fighting.

"Yeah," she said. "Yeah, he's here."

****

Just a few short hours ago, Trip had actually complained to himself that small-town life was tedious.

His heart had jumped in his chest when the door slammed itself, but her body had relaxed in his arms. She'd regained her footing while he stared open-mouthed at the door, and he made no move to resist when she stepped away from him.

"That…was your husband?" he asked.

She turned to face him and nodded. "His name is Cameron."

"And Cameron is here. Now."

"That's right." She regarded him with a serene expression that he couldn't quite read. Either she'd resigned herself to whatever response he would have, or she knew she had him.

Maybe it was both. He could no longer successfully argue that this Cameron didn't exist, not after he'd forced his way into his body downstairs. Not after he'd trapped the two of them up here in the bedroom. If he could do that, then he could do whatever was necessary to make sure Trip was here to stay. As long as he was needed. And if things didn't go so well, it was clear Cameron wasn't afraid to use force.

She sat down on the bed and scooted over to the far edge, clutching the sheets as if they'd never seen each other. His knees crackled when he bent to pick his boxer shorts out of the pile of clothes on the floor. He rose on unsteady legs to put them on, and when he was done, she patted the bed next to her. The lamp she'd grabbed a moment ago had upset a small framed picture. He'd noticed it before. In the dark, he'd made out only her shape and that of a man, and then he'd tried to ignore it. She hadn't mentioned a husband, so he'd decided the man in the picture was a brother or a father or some other man whose image would interfere with his enjoyment of her.

Gently, she picked up the little frame, the sort of uncomplicated thing one found in a drugstore near the boxes of envelopes, and she gave it to him. Now Trip saw him, a tall, lanky fellow who held her close as they both smiled for the camera. Horn-rimmed glasses and black hair cut in a flat top. So this was Cameron.

He turned to her as he joined her on the bed. "This is him?" Trip asked.

"Yeah."

He looked like the kind of man who loved the structure and routine of marriage. Someone who took out the trash without needing to be nagged. Someone who washed his own dishes and clothes. Like someone who loved being part of a team and doing his part to make sure they both reached their fullest potential. He looked like a good husband.

She sat back, leaning against the headboard. He handed her the photo in its cheap goldtone frame.

"How long were you married?"

"Two months. We were together a lot longer than that, but we were only married for two months."

He glanced over at her. Her large eyes were locked to the photo, and she'd gone very still on the bed. Her hand rose slowly from her lap to cover her mouth, and when it shuddered there, he leaned over toward her, ready to hold her when she began to cry. But she took a deep breath, letting it straighten her spine as she inhaled.

"We had just moved in here. We wanted to have a housewarming party—well, I wanted it—but Halloween was his favorite holiday. We decided to have a costume party instead."

A tear slid down her cheek, over smooth sepia skin. But her voice was steady. Maybe she'd finally told this story so many times that she could do it without weeping.

He wondered how many times that was, exactly.

He touched her knee, partly to reassure her that he wasn't so much angry as confused, and partly to urge her to continue.

"I had a Cleopatra costume. You know, the standard outfit with the dress and the stupid little snake bracelet and everything. Except it didn't have the beaded headdress. You know, the one that goes like this." She brushed her fingers down over her sex-rumpled black hair to mimic the strands of beads.

"Yeah, I know."

"I didn't need it." She shrugged. "It was obviously Cleopatra. And he was going to be Marc Antony, and everyone would get it. I didn't need anything else. I just really *wanted* it. It was so pretty. I was lucky to get the costume; the deluxe ones always sell out, and I waited til the last minute for it. But of course the head thing was sold out."

She took another deep breath. Another tear welled in her bottomless brown eyes. He reached out to brush it away, but she took his hand and squeezed it.

"It's okay. It's all right." She sighed and rested their joined hands on her thigh, next to the photo on her lap. "The house was crowded before I started to think it was taking him a long time to get back." She looked up at him. "Everyone was asking where he was. Where's Cam? But I didn't wonder where he was for a long time, until he was the only one missing. That's when I got the phone call."

This part of the story came slowly. The part about the accident. A sober driver on a clear day, shooting through a red light into his car. Plastic beads all over the front seat. Sound spiraling away as she realized that this was real and not a horrible prank she'd never, ever forgive. The phone sliding from her hand. The way she'd opened her mouth, expecting to puke, only to have a scream come gurgling out instead.

Still raw, especially tonight. Trip wanted to spare her this account of the worst day of her life, but it seemed wrong to do that. Disrespectful to the husband who was still here between them.

"I'm sorry," he said.

"I am, too. He'd have liked you. He had a way of meeting all kinds of different people." She chuckled. "In the grocery line. Locker room at the gym. Cop pulled him over once and ended up being a groomsman." She sighed and let her head drop backward until she looked up at the ceiling. "It's been six years. Sometimes it sneaks up on you."

"Like tonight."

"Yeah." She released his hand. "I went to that bar the first time because I didn't want to go home. I couldn't go home. You know, the memory was just more…present than usual. I didn't know what I was doing, aside from having a drink to make it easier to sleep that night. But then I met someone there. Joey. We closed the bar that night. We were there for six hours, and I didn't think about this even once. I wanted to take him home just because of that."

"Was that the first time?"

She nodded. "Yeah. I didn't know it at first. I just knew it felt peaceful and right." She looked at him and pressed her full, rosy lips together, like she was trying to decide how much to say. She looked down at the photo. "Later that night…, afterwards, I woke up, and he was looking at me." She shifted her weight on the bed and looked up at him. "I saw a movie once where the guy and the girl were separated by magic—they never actually see each other except for this one freak moment. And when it happens, he just stares at her. Like he's holding his breath. Like the slightest move will break the spell." She sighed and traced Cam's face in the photo. "I knew. Cam was *in* there. Looking at me. And he said he was sorry. He said, 'I'm so sorry, DJ.'"

"His name for you?" Trip asked.

"He knew I hated it," she said. A smile brightened her features. "But he was the only one who used it. I think he knew I wouldn't believe it was him otherwise."

After a pause, he asked, "And then what?"

"I went off on him. Not because I didn't think it was him. I knew it was, somehow. But…" She bit her lip, and when she spoke again, tears choked her voice. "He *left* me here. We were *together*. And then he was gone." She sniffled and rubbed her eyes. "Part of me wanted to be happy that Cam was here now, that he'd come back like this and we could be together. And part of me really hated him for putting me in this position. We were part of each other."

"And then he was gone." Trip eased over on the bed until their hips were touching and put his arm around her shoulders.

She nodded. "It felt good to really yell at him. Just let it all out. At the end, he held me really tight, and I cried and cried." She took a deep, unsteady breath and patted Trip's hand. "As sure as I had been that Cam was right here that night, the next morning, I was just as sure he was gone. I was sure this guy, Joey, would say something about how I had freaked out, or he'd run off because it was so awkward and weird."

"But what? Nothing?"

She shook her head. "I think he knew something had happened that he didn't totally remember, but nothing he couldn't blame on a night of drinking." She blushed. "The next Halloween, almost to celebrate, I did it again."

"Was it just as good that time?"

"Yeah." She stopped, becoming thoughtful. "The next time, I knew. I just knew he was *in* there. It never felt crazy. After Joey, it made perfect, perfect sense. And so I called him Cam and we just went on like that all night." She carefully wiped her tears with her fingertips. "We made love, and we talked until the sun came up. And at the end, he said goodbye. 'I gotta go. He's coming back.'"

"So this is your night with him? With Cameron?"

She nodded and swallowed more tears. "Well, not really. This is the first time we've done it this way. I wanted more time, I guess. I didn't think it through."

"Wait. This is the first time what way?"

"Usually, we do it Halloween night." She sniffled.

He frowned. "But tonight's the thirtieth."

"It *was*. Now it's Halloween." She grinned shyly.

"Ohh. So it's like getting two nights."

"And all day in between, maybe. If it had worked."

She put the photo back on the nightstand next to her. "Maybe not the whole day. We might just have been in and out for as long as you were willing to stay. Like I said, I didn't think it through very well."

He kissed her temple, where her fine hair was fragrant. "Is this the first time things have gone wrong?"

She nodded. "Yeah. Usually, he just slides in and out and the other guy doesn't really know. Wakes up feeling weird. Blames the alcohol. No real harm done."

"How sad." He drew up his knees and rested his arms on them. "Don't you think?"

"Is it?" She faced him, her brow furrowed. "Fewer questions that way. I don't know if you've noticed, but this has the potential for a lot of questions."

"Don't you want questions? Don't you want to really share the experience?" He turned to her, his shoulder against the headboard. "Have you ever thought that this would be easier if you didn't have to find a new person every time?"

She chuckled and patted his knee. "See, this is why I chose you. Not everyone is open-minded like you, you know. How am I going to manage to find one person for this every year?"

"You'd be surprised. People are into some very interesting things in a small town like this. This started off wrong when Cam basically assaulted me downstairs."

She looked up at him. "Would you have stayed? If I'd told you?"

"It depends on how you'd told me." He tucked some of her hair behind her ear. "I would probably have expected candles or a ritual with chanting or something. What actually happened wasn't as complicated."

She slapped his shoulder playfully, and they both laughed.

"I mean, Cam can teach me how to please you. You might find something new that you like with me. Each year, all three people grow into it. Each year is better. And you wouldn't have to find a new person every year. Yeah, I'd sign on for that."

"You are…wait." She turned toward him. "You are willing to let Cam have your body for this?"

"Yeah. I mean, don't get me wrong. It is definitely weird to have someone else in your body. But for you… for the way you were with him…and the sensation of it…yeah. I'm willing. At least for now."

"Really? You would do that for us?"

He nodded. "Cam and I have gotten to know each other now, right? What was it you said? He made friends wherever he went? Besides, I like to finish what I start."

She threw her arms around his shoulders, and when her tears wet his skin, he held her tight as she cried.

Not fighting Cam made the process much easier.

He'd moved to the edge of the bed to undress, not wanting to be close to her. The memory of struggling with Cam was fresh, of stretching and trying to shake and throw him off. He hadn't wanted to throw an elbow or a shoulder without meaning to.

She'd reassured him that it was unnecessary, that if he wasn't resisting Cam would just slide into him the way he might slide into an overcoat. But she'd never actually seen it happen, peacefully or not, and he couldn't rely on her word. For all she knew, there was no gentle way.

Downstairs, he'd only had a moment to sense Cam before he invaded and took over, just a few instants to realize that this was no pesky insect, no nascent muscle cramp. Cam's presence had brushed against him, tentatively at first, before wrapping itself over and around him, down over his shoulders, something shapeless and strong grappling with him. He had nothing to strike at, nothing to grip, and it had deepened its embrace, flattening itself over his spine, reaching around his ribs and then into him. It had crushed the breath from him, coiling around him like a snake and forcing out one last gasp. After that, he was a passenger, at the mercy of this voiceless force.

This time felt almost the same. Weight and pressure descending over him, around him. His head swam and he wanted to hang on to something. He swayed.

Hold on there, buddy. Just hold still.

"Cam?"

Yeah. Who'd you expect?

Pressure squeezed his rib cage, and he fought the urge to breathe in, inflate his chest, to repel him.

Almost there. Hold on.

Then he released his breath and felt normal again. No weird pressure. Nothing but the strange sensation that someone else was in his head. He didn't feel invaded or violated. It was as if his flesh were a vehicle, and he were sitting in its cockpit with a stranger, trying to decide who would fly it.

Okay. All done.

"Done?" he asked, mostly seeking reassurance that they wouldn't have to fight again. Deirdre's face brightened and he smiled back at her.

Yeah. You don't have to keep talking. Now that I'm in here, I can hear you thinking.

Okay. That was weird. In a way, just like any other mental conversation he'd ever had with himself over which beer to buy or what to watch, but with someone else, whose responses he couldn't predict.

She doesn't need to hear everything. Right?

An oily chill skittered over him at the thought of keeping secrets from the woman he'd shared so much with. "What do you mean?" He couldn't imagine how he'd stop Cam if he turned on them both, now that he was in here, but if it meant protecting her from harm, Trip would let Cam kill him.

Don't be like that. If anyone were going to get hurt here, it'd be you. You didn't get that from last time?

"So what do you mean?" Trip asked.

A pause just long enough for a sigh. *I want to thank you. Man to man. You didn't have to do any of this.*

Trip smiled. *Were you here for all of it?*

Everything after midnight.

Okay. Trip's skin prickled. How much had Cam seen?

I have an idea what you all did, but just an idea. Don't worry. If it weren't pretty special, you wouldn't still be here. And believe it or not, this isn't what I wanted to talk about.

"Are you talking?" she asked.

Concentrating on a real conversation and the one in his head was harder than he'd expected, and Trip nodded, lifting one finger to hold her off.

I'm just trying to thank you. Especially for what you said earlier. I know this must be weird.

That doesn't start to cover it, Cameron. But you're

welcome. She's...she loves you. Still. Very much.

Another sigh-long pause. *I love her, too. Being with her was the only thing in my life that mattered. That only sounds crazy to you now because you haven't been there yet. All that shit about saying you love her every day is true.*

"What's he saying?" she asked.

Don't tell her. I'll tell her in a minute.

"It's good," said Trip. "I promise."

They looked at each other for a few long seconds.

How should we—

I'll take it from here. You should relax and enjoy.

He crawled across the bed to her. His body moved of its own accord.

She gazed at him, her body relaxing for the first time since he'd fought to regain control of himself. "You back?"

"Yeah, baby." Trip felt his mouth moving, heard his voice as Cam spoke through him. "I'm back."

She slipped her arms around him. Her face softened into a bright, open smile, a welcome meant for her mate. "He's great, isn't he?"

"Best one yet."

Thanks again, buddy. Cam's voice felt warm inside his mind.

Deirdre lay back in bed and pulled him down toward her. *Don't mention it.*

Giving up control of his body wasn't the hard part. It was just like going limp, relaxing before sleep. The tough part was letting someone else take control, drive his body as if he were an elaborate toy.

But she made it easier.

She caressed him, like she was trying to explore every inch of his body, the curve of each muscle, the warmth of his skin. He knelt over her and watched desire bloom on her face as her fingertips slid over his flat stomach. His cock stiffened and swelled, and she stroked its length. The memory of her soft, lush lips around his shaft made him ache before she released him and moved on to fondle his thigh.

"That feels good," Cam said to her.

"Does it?" Her voice was teasing.

"Yeah." He lowered himself onto his elbows and she reached for him. He caught her hands, laced his fingers with hers, and pinned her hands to the mattress. She squirmed beneath him and purred.

"He's kind of built for this," he said. "Don't you think?"

"He is." She kissed him eagerly, flicking his tongue with hers before he claimed her fiercely with his mouth. "He's not so sure of it."

Built for what? What were they talking about?

Cam ignored his confusion. "He's like a machine," he said. "He knows where you're going to go next."

He could anticipate her next move, sure. But Cam was searching his mind for something deeper, instinctive.

"Mm-hmm," she said. "Come here."

Cam lowered himself onto her, and she cradled him between her thighs. He released one of her hands long enough to yank the sheet away from her, baring her full, round breasts. She gasped.

"Oh, God," she whispered. "Come here."

He kissed her again, pushing her mouth open with his and taking her with his tongue. He let his hand snake into her hair and he made a fist in it before pulling it hard.

She opened her legs a little wider and he shifted his weight on top of her, using his body to trap and restrain her. A sound, something guttural and coarse, issued from him, something he'd never heard before.

He sucked her lower lip hard and bit it before starting a trail of kisses over her jaw. He clenched the fist in her hair.

"You like that?" Cam asked. And he knew damn well she did. She loved it. He loved to hear it and she loved to say it.

She wanted to be taken, to be at his mercy. She

wanted to feel his strength in opposition to hers. She wanted to struggle with him, her arousal mounting as he claimed her.

"Yeah," she whispered.

A surge of pleasure shot through him. How strange, just to be along for the ride. His cock ached, and as much as he wanted to be inside her, slowly working her to another climax, Cam had other ideas.

He palmed her breast, rubbing the center of his hand over her nipple until it came to a hard peak. He grabbed at her hard and sucked viciously at her throat. Her nails dug into his shoulders, but he barely registered the sting before she grabbed a fistful of his hair and yanked it.

The sensation of pain slid down his spine like an electric current and his cock pulsed with need. The sheet tangled around her waist, separating them, and he longed to tear it away and bury himself inside her.

Not yet.

He returned his attention to her luscious tits, greedily feasting on her. He grazed her soft skin with his teeth, and some perverse part of Trip wanted Cam to leave a mark on her, a sign that she was his and would always belong to him.

A sound of delight rolled out of her, and she arched and twisted beneath him. "Yes."

"Damn." He lifted himself off her until he was kneeling again. "I need to be inside you."

She struggled to free her legs from the sheet, and he took hold of her delicate ankles, lifting her legs over her head, exposing the slick, swollen folds of her. He rested her legs against his shoulders and braced himself against the headboard before ramming himself into her.

She'd been a snug fit for him before, and he'd eased into her then, savoring every inch of her until her innermost muscles fluttered around him, almost triggering his climax before he'd wanted. Now, with her hips lifted up toward him, her channel was even tighter, and while his own instincts screamed that he should take her slowly, the need, the naked hunger contorting her features made him surrender to her husband's primal drives.

That first savage thrust had nearly been his undoing; high voltage pleasure rocked him to his core. He ground his teeth to settle himself, and the dark delight of it took over as he pumped viciously into her with long, forceful strokes. For a time there was nothing but sensation. The impossibly tight heat of her pussy. Her face, at once relaxed and greedy for more, her eyes squeezed closed as she cried out. White teeth bared as she gasped lustful demands. More. Deeper. Harder.

"God," she cried. "Fuck me harder."

He lost himself in it. More than he'd ever done before, he gave himself over to the savagery of it and fucked her harder and deeper than he'd dared that night, and she reveled in it.

Her climax began deep inside her, where hidden muscles closed around his cock as he buried himself to the hilt in her. When she came, seizing him inside her, his own climax coiled at the base of his cock, twisting tightly there until he let go. His body seemed to unfurl and release, and for a moment, he felt like little more than a conduit made of flesh, the medium she used to claim her mate one more time.

Then it was over, and the electric jolt of ecstasy was gone. Everything that had driven him gave way. He held himself above her on quivering arms, and he watched her return to herself, catching her breath. She pressed her fingertips to her glistening forehead. An ecstatic glow lit her satiny skin from within.

They thanked him at the same time, her voice and her husband's becoming one in his head and heart. He had just enough strength left to nod and lower her legs to the bed again before collapsing onto the mattress.

Trip woke with his eyes open. He was positioned on his side, his arm tucked under the pillow. He was troubled by the odd sensation that he'd interrupted a conversation with himself.

"He's waking up," Cam said with his voice.

She kissed his forehead. "Thanks," she said. "Thank you, Trip."

Trip kissed her cheek. He was barely able to summon the will to lift himself from the pillow, and everything in him wanted to go back to sleep. Hell, Cam could talk to her as much as he wanted, as long as he could sleep.

"I think we used him up," Cam said.

She chuckled and patted his shoulder. "Me too."

Trip tried to figure out if she meant she agreed with Cameron, that she also felt depleted, or both. He spent what felt like a long time on that before wanting to sleep again.

"Can I stay?" he asked.

"Yeah," she said. "Of course. We've got a whole day ahead of us."

I wasn't planning on going anywhere.

Neither was I, Cam. Trip shook his head feebly. *You still ask.*

I guess so. Go to sleep. I was having a private conversation.

You have a hell of a nerve. Trip chuckled. *I wish I'd met you before. Which would be the only thing in the world that could make this weirder.*

"What's he saying?" she asked.

"I'll tell you in a second," Cam said. "He's almost asleep. Happy Halloween."

Sleep began to overtake Trip as Deirdre chuckled. "Trick or treat, Trip. Or both."

The Timeshare Trip

by

Renci Denham

The cruise ship traversed the clear blue waters off the coast of Costa Rica at a leisurely pace. The gentle wind tousled the hair of the passengers lounging around in cut-off jean shorts and swim suits. It was perfect weather for such an occasion, warm but not hot. The morning sun beamed down upon the passengers. Cotton-ball clouds floated lazily by in a crystal-blue sky.

Crystal smiled at her husband, Roy, sitting in the lounge chair next to hers. "Ah, this is the place to be in October!" She sat up, jutting out her large double-D bosoms. "Don't you like my new bikini?"

Roy scrunched his eyebrows together. "How much did you pay for that?"

"Oh, don't be such a cheapskate, Roy. I got it at the swap meet for five bucks!"

"Well, that's five bucks too much. I could have made you one out of duct tape."

Roy grinned, displaying brown, crooked teeth. "You're right about the weather. Back home it's chilly as all get-out. Here I can show off my great bod with no shirt and in my shorts!" Roy flexed his muscled arms. "Look at that, girly. Doesn't that just make you want to jump my bones right now?"

His long, stringy brown hair would fall in his face when the wind blew in the wrong direction. He pushed a few greasy strands behind his ear, then reached for the bowl of tortilla chips sitting on the table beside him and grabbed up a handful. He shoved the mass in his mouth all at once. *Crunch! Smack!* Tortilla-laden spittle dribbled down his chin with each chew.

"I can't believe we won a free cruise!" Crystal said. "And a Halloween cruise with a big costume party at the end to beat that!"

"So what kind of costume for the big Halloween bash did you get?"

"Oh, it's a surprise! What about you?"

"Oh, it's a surprise too. I'm telling you though, it will make every woman there want to jump my bones."

Crystal rolled her eyes but said nothing. She reached over to the table beside her lounge chair and grabbed a claw hair clip. She twisted her long bleached-blonde hair on top of her head, creating a fountain effect. Her eyes were as blue as the sky, but she was pushing thirty-five, and too much booze, too much tanning and too many unpaid bills were starting to carve lines in her face. "I always hear of people winning." She continued, "Like Cathy Moore, my cousin, won three days in Branson once. But a full-week, all-inclusive cruise in Costa Rico! Yee haw! I never thought anything like that would happen to us!"

Roy looked at his wife of three months and scratched his behind. "Costa Rico, that's part of Mexico, right? Now, that all-inclusive does include drinks, right? And I don't mean no coffee or tea. I mean beer and whisky." He scratched his testicles. "Who's Cathy Moore?"

Crystal slapped her husband's arm. "God darn it, Roy, I said my cousin! And could you try chewing with your mouth closed? We'z with classy folk now! Act like you weren't raised in a trailer park. Why, look at that pool on the deck below us. I ain't never seen anything like it. It's a real pool, not one of those blow-up kinds, and it's on a boat."

"Well, does it include beer, woman?"

A slim, dark-haired waitress with a tray of beverages suddenly appeared. "May I offer you a beverage?"

Crystal's eyes got huge and her mouth dropped

open. She pointed at a fresh pineapple cut open with a beverage inside. The concoction was garnished with bananas and cherries. "What is that?"

"That is a piña colada."

"Those are free, right?"

The waitress tipped her head.

Crystal continued to stare at the pineapple. "Does it have alcohol in it?"

The waitress again was silent but tipped her head.

"I'm going to have me one of those there piña coladas then."

"Damn it, woman! Don't go putting on airs. I was raised in a trailer park and I will die in a trailer park. Damn proud of it, too! Our children will probably be raised in a trailer park, too. As fer you moving into my trailer, it's a mighty big step up for you after livin' in that there house of your mama's! I know you had to chop up firewood for the wood stove. At least now you got heat! Now answer me before I slap you upside the head. Who is Cathy Moore?"

Crystal rolled her eyes. "You know, my cousin Linda's daughter-in-law. The one with the triplets."

Roy took a gander at his wife. "Didn't I tell you to stay away from that woman Linda? She's always puttin' thoughts in your head about going back to school and being high falutin'. Like she has room to talk. Those grandbabies of hers look like they were born outside the nuclear power plant."

Crystal scowled at her husband. "They ain't high falutin' ideas. Her daughter-in-law went back to school for six weeks, and now she works in a nursing home as a real nursing assistant." She slapped her knee and giggled. "Those kids are scary lookin', though. That one has that crooked eye; it's always movin' all over the place. I don't know what it's lookin' at!"

Roy lifted his leg and let out a loud fart. "Damn, I hope they serve us something other than chili at this here resort. I have enough gas from that dinner we ate last night to power this here cruise ship." He finally shoved the last of the chips in his mouth and chewed them up.

Crystal slapped her husband's arm so hard, a loud crack resounded. "Damn it, Roy, I told you to chew with your mouth closed. We are with fancy people now."

"You gonna let her get away with that?"

Crystal and Roy looked up at a rotund figure standing over them.

Roy's eyes moved to the white belly that hung over the man's bright yellow swim trunks, and he rubbed his own buff arms, his palm lingering over the prison tattoos to make sure the other man saw them.

"Well, sir, I would smack her around a little, but I

don't know my own strength." He clenched his fists to flex his muscles a little. "As you can see I've done some hard time. The last time I did that, I knocked out two of her teeth. Show 'em, Crystal girl."

Crystal took off her flip-flop and held it in a boomerang grip like she was about to chuck it at him, but she put the shoe back on her foot and shot Roy the side eye.

"Go on, don't be shy. Show 'em."

Crystal huffed, then leaned forward and put her forefingers in her mouth. She stretched the corners of her lips to expose the two missing molars in the back.

Roy beamed. "That there shows what happens when a real man doesn't know his own strength." He stood up and flexed his pecs. "Yes sirree, I sure as shittin' learned my lesson that day. Don't go about beatin' your wife, 'cause the next time it might be a front tooth. Lord knows if she loses her front teeth, I can't go showin' her off in public."

Roy moved to stand behind his wife. He leaned over and wrapped his arms around her breasts, pushing them up over the black spandex bikini. He grinned. "This is more than the bitch was wearin' when I rescued her from working in a nudie bar." He made a fist and rubbed the knuckles across her head.

"Darn it, Roy. Haven't I told you not to go tellin'

people we met at the Club X? I'm a married woman now. I don't want people to know what I used to do for a livin.'" Crystal raised her chin. "I'm a real waitress in a real restaurant now. I mean, people come in and sit down and everything." She brushed a loose strand of hair from her face and tried to shove it back in the clip. "When we get back to Missouri, I'm goin' back to school and work in a nursing home."

Roy patted his wife on the head and glared at the man still blocking the sun. "That's my little lady. She's always dreamin' big!"

As the man smiled, sweat dripped down his face into his mouth. He spit it out, making his three chins jiggle. "Well, good to meet you two. I'm Bruce." Bruce raised his arm and pointed at a large women snoozing in a lounge chair. The flab under his arm wiggled. "That there is my fine lady, Sally."

"Good Lord, I don't know when the last time I saw a woman's rear hang off a chair like that."

Bruce glowed. "Yes sirree, bub! I can afford to keep my wife in style!"

Roy shook his head and muttered under his breath, "I'm glad my woman knows how to control herself." He craned his neck toward the big man. "Good Lord there, Bruce, all I can see is a ring of sunlight around your body. It's like looking at one of those eclipses or some'n!

Ya mind movin' to the side there a little? I need to work on my tan."

"Sorry, bub," Bruce muttered as he shuffled off to the side. He ran his fingers through his stringy comb-over. "How did y'all wind up here? This seems like a pricy place."

Roy beamed. "My little lady here entered us in a contest at the supermarket. Sure, we have to sit through one of those timeshare presentations, but it's at the very end so we can have a blast until then." He shook his head. "Now, we've been to plenty of them timeshare things, and they never are what they say they are. One time they said we won a free grill and it was nothin' but an aluminum foil pie-tin with some charcoal in it. When they first called, I told Crystal here it was another scam, but I went on the internet at the library and saw the resort. I said to Crystal, 'Crystal, they're paying for the bus to Florida, so what the Hell, we'll go and check it out, and if'n the cruise ship looks as good as it does on that there video screen, we are goin' on board.'

"Sure enough, we got to the docks and the cruise ship was real! Seven days and six nights, all we can eat and drink! That's worth settin' through a timeshare presentation at the end. If'n they do push us to sign the papers, it's not like our credit will go through anyway!"

Bruce laughed. "That's pretty much what I said

to Sally over there. I told her she was full of shit when she told me we won, but we live in Jacksonville so we drove to the docks, and there as plain as the nose on my face, the ship was real. So I figure the rest of the trip is real too." Bruce whipped a stray booger away from his nostril. The ship's horn blew, gaining the attention of all. "Well, lookie there. There's the land and there's the resort sittin' right on the beach, just like it shows in the picture!"

Roy and Crystal leaned up and raised their hands to their foreheads to shade their eyes from the noonday sun.

The resort—a single story of pink adobe—nestled like a secret palace in the lush green fauna of the Costa Rican jungle. Turrets encrusted with sapphire tiles sparkled at each corner.

Colorful birds perched in the trees—some chirped, some squeaked and some had learned English.

One parrot hopped from branch to branch screeching, "Uh-oh, you're in trouble." A hyacinth macaw squawked, "Oh, this is going to be fun!"

Crystal jumped up and clapped her hands together.

"Gosh dern it, woman! Quit bouncing around like that. Those boobs of yours are flying all over the place. They're already starting to sag and that just makes them worse!"

The cruise ship pulled up to the street right in front of the building and docked. The engines continued to hum.

Roy pinched Crystal's ass. "Feel that vibration, baby. Maybe you might want to do a split on the deck before we leave."

Without responding to her husband, Crystal grabbed the plain purple sarong she had been laying on and tied it around her waist.

The ship's captain came from the main cabin and greeted the guests. His white captain's uniform was impeccably clean and pressed. "Good morning to all of you. I apologize for not making my acquaintance earlier, but I have had to see to the running of the ship. Allow me to personally escort you off the ship."

"You do take your job seriously, don't ya? Why, if'n I didn't know better, I would think I was a hog being herded off to slaughter," Bruce spouted.

"Indeed, the safe arrival of my passengers is most serious to me." The captain gestured toward the resort. "Please follow me."

"Come on, woman." Roy slapped Crystal on her rump. "The man said to follow him, so stop your slack-jaw starin'. Get your behind moving and follow him."

The quests and the captain strode off the boat and through the gates of the adobe palace into a courtyard.

Slap, slap, slap echoed against the walls as the quests' flip-flops moved across heavy terra cotta tiles. Colorful paintings of tropical scenery graced the blush-pink walls. Exotic plants were strategically placed throughout the courtyard, some hanging from the ceilings.

"Lookie here, Roy, at this plant. Looks like one of them water lilies. My cousin Linda tried growin' one of these but it ended up poisoning her cat."

"Well, that cat of hers is almost as dumb as her kids."

A clerk dressed in a crisp white shirt and khaki slacks manned the front desk. He looked up from his paperwork to eyeball the guests, and then focused back onto the stacks of paper in front of him. Beige overstuffed furniture sat in conversation groups throughout the lounge. Waiters dressed in white shirts and colorful Bermuda shorts scurried through a set of double wooden doors into the lobby and presented trays of assorted beverages—bottles of numerous beers, glasses of wine, both red and white, a pink rum punch in fancy glass cups and piña coladas in pineapples.

Crystal clapped her hands and jumped up and down again, her boobs flying all over the place. "They have those there piña coladas! Whooie, I'm gonna have me a good time!" She ran over and plucked a piña colada off the tray, nearly knocking down the waiter.

Roy followed her, grabbing a beer. "Well, don't go getting too used to it, woman. A hot dog at the quick store is still Friday dinner out when we get back home."

Bruce and the other vacationers elbowed in, scarfing up drinks. "Move over, boy," the fat man said as he snatched a beer for his other hand. "I plan on being a two-fisted drinker while I'm here."

Roy eyeballed the man and rubbed his prison tats.

Crystal slapped her husband. "Now, don't go startin' a fight and gettin' us kicked off the island. We're still barred from the quick mart by our house because of the last brawl you got into. Anytime we want a Friday night dinner out, we have to go five miles down the road now."

A tall, slender man with dark hair and dark eyes strode up to the vacationers. His skin was a clear mocha; his hair was neatly trimmed and combed back. He was dressed in a white shirt and tan khakis. Sharp edges creased both the legs of the pants and the sleeves of his shirt. "I am Edwardo. I am the resort manager, and I am here if you need assistance."

"Edwardo," Roy said, exaggerating the second syllable of the man's name. "Ain't he a fancy one? Edwardo." Roy giggled so loud he let out a snort. "I bet those pant legs are what they use to cut off the tops of those pineapples. I bet Edwardo has never done any hard time! Okay, I finished my beer, so I'm gonna try one of those fancy drinks with an umbrella in it. I've always seen them on the TV but have never got one before."

"Well, don't go getting all high falutin," Crystal said.

Roy raised his hand as if to hit her, then pulled it back. "Gosh dern it, woman! Don't go ruining this for me. I'm here to have a good time, not listen to your mouth!"

Bruce waved at the waiters. "Come on! You hurry it up with another tray. You said all I can drink, and I haven't had all I can drink!"

Sally threw her head back and emptied her beer bottle in a long gulp. "Aren't you proud of me, baby? I can drink almost as much as you!"

"That's my little woman. I sure am proud of her," Bruce said to Roy. "She gets plenty of practice at home. As I said, I can afford to keep my little lady in style."

Roy put his arm around Crystal, pushing up her boobs. He let out a smirk as he brushed a greasy lock behind his ear. 'Little woman'? 'Little' woman if'n you're comparing her to a Mack truck." He turned back to the waiters. "The man's right about one thing, keep 'em comin.'"

The waiters ran back and forth between the lobby and double doors that led to the kitchen, keeping the drinks flowing. The passengers still swarmed around the waiters, competing for a beverage. Attempting to keep the crowd under control, Edwardo motioned for the waiters to stand by the kitchen and began passing out drinks from the trays, one at a time.

Roy grabbed a drink from Edwardo and leaned in toward Crystal. "The only problem I see here is all the Mexicans. At least they know their place here! When I said keep 'em comin', they kept 'em comin.'" He drew deeply on the straw and swallowed, then grabbed his forehead. "Damn! Brain freeze! Come here, boy, and give me another one of those things!"

"I thought you was only gonna drink beer and whiskey, Roy," Crystal said.

"Hush your mouth, woman. You're gonna embarrass me." He waved at Edwardo. "Hand me another of those damn things. I'z plan to get drunk!"

A beautiful woman entered the room from double doors in the back and glided toward them. She appeared to be in her mid-thirties, with tan skin that was clear and smooth, but she had an air of wisdom and confidence about her that a younger woman might not possess. Dark hair, glistening like obsidian in the sunlight shining through the large windows, touched her rump and swayed as she moved. She smiled. Her eyes were dark and wide open, her pupils huge, giving the effect of a doe-eyed seductress of royal descent. She wore a long purple-flowered halter dress, the epitome of affluent resort wear. She raised her slender arm to motion them forward. "I am Carmen, your hostess. Please join me for a quick tour. Come this way."

She led them through the lobby and into an adjacent open building. A thatched roof over the building protected the party from the increasingly hot sun. Gentle breezes scented of florals from the jungle and salt air flowed through the room.

The woman smiled again and gestured to a table with her right hand. "This is the buffet. As you can see, there is any food you could possibly imagine. We have both local and imported cheeses, local fruits, and a fresh rack of lamb in a chipotle sauce, just to name a few. Really, I cannot imagine you wanting for anything while you stay with us. Please take all you want but eat all you take!"

Roy eyed the table of food. "What, no ribs? What is that chipotle shit? I thought you would have some good, old-fashioned ribs!"

Crystal smacked Roy's arm. "Really, Roy!"

"What, woman? I'm here on vacation. Do you know how much ribs are at the diner down the road?"

Carmen smiled. "Sir, if it is ribs you want, it is ribs you will get. Just let us know and give us the time to prepare them for you. Until then, I am sure you will find plenty of food that pleases you on the buffet." She gave a sweeping motion with her left arm. "Now please, follow me."

She pointed to the left. "The pools are over there." Three large pools of crystal-clear water were laid out on a hill in a step-like pattern.

Crystal's mouth dropped open. "Good Lord, Roy, they have a rock waterfall and everything!"

Roy grinned. "Hot damn! There are three of them! And look at that a swim-up bar!" Roy squeezed his wife at the waist. "Come on, baby, let's eat! I do see something I want. I'm getting me one of those there lobsters." His nostrils flared as he turned toward one of the waiters standing by a tray of drinks. "Come on, boy! Give me another one of those! Damn lazy Mexicans."

The waiter lowered his head, picked up the tray, walked over to Roy and presented the beverages. If Roy hadn't been so focused on the buffet, the booze and his wife's double-D breasts, he would have noticed the slight smile that graced the waiter's face.

The lot gorged themselves. Bruce and Roy soon became friends.

"Okay, I've eaten all I can eat." Roy lifted his rump and cut loose. He glanced around until he spotted Edwardo, then flagged him. "I need go somewhere private to take care of some private business, if'n you know what I mean."

"Of course, sir." Edwardo snapped his fingers and a waiter sprinted forward. "This is Juan. He will show you to your room."

Roy and Crystal stood and followed Juan down a meandering path around some more jungle flora. Birds sang around them, some speaking. "Uh-oh, you're in trouble." They continued on the path until they reached their room. It had an extra-king-sized bed and a huge set of sliding-glass doors that opened up onto the beach.

The week flew by. The couple slept in their massive bed with its soft feather mattress, down pillows and comfy covers that warmed them during the chilly Central American nights. The sliding-glass doors kept the room cool during the hot days but allowed the aromatic breezes to flow. Just as in the lobby, colorful paintings of local flora and street scenes graced the walls. Each day, housekeeping staff placed fresh flowers on the night table. The room smelled of tropical flowers and Roy's farts.

During the days, the couple lounged by the pool, drinking massive amounts of piña coladas served in real pineapples, and tequila sunrises. They partied and partied some more. One night Crystal threw up from the excess. She tried to make it to the bushes, but she lost it on the sidewalk between the buffet and the swimming pools.

Roy snorted at her. "Girl, that there is just alcohol abuse. That's what that is." He looked up at the night sky. Between the lights of the torches and the huge full moon, it was almost as light as day. "Yes sirree, this is a fine place. Yep, said it before and I'll say it again. Seems to me the only thing wrong with Mexico is all the damn Mexicans. Edwardo—whooie!—isn't he just full of himself? Edwaaardo…"

Roy swatted at his cheek when a breeze grazed the side of his face. He flinched when a shadow passed overhead, then stared up at the sky. "Good Lord, the birds sure get big here." He smiled and grabbed his crotch. "Not as big as this though! Come on, woman. We›z got some partying to do!"

"Oh, Roy, I don't think I can eat or drink any more. I just threw up all over the place."

"Well, that just means you have an empty stomach and can start all over again!"

****

The night of the Halloween party, Roy and Crystal readied themselves in their room. Roy removed his costume from its plastic bag, pulled on the tight black pants and shirt, and finally pulled the black stocking facemask over his head. Once the costume was fully in place, he put his hands on his hips and preened in front of the mirror. He turned toward Crystal and pointed at his face. "Look at me, woman. Alls you can see is my eyes."

He turned back toward the mirror, flexing his muscles. Each flex threatened to tear the costume's cheap polyester fabric. He peeked around to see if Crystal noticed. She was fussing with her apron, so he stomped his foot. "Crystal, look at me."

Crystal looked up at him but said nothing.

"Look at me, Crystal, I'm a ninja!" He lunged toward her. "I'm ninja fast, and I'm gonna get you!" He leapt around the bed and grabbed her below the chest, squeezing her breasts together. He kissed her neck, slobbering all over it.

Crystal pushed Roy off. "You're ninja fast, all right, if'n ya know what I mean. Anyway, don't mess up my costume."

Roy eyeballed his wife. She was wearing a thigh-high ruffled dress made out of the same cheap black polyester. She also had on a ruffled apron and cap made from the same fabric but in white. "Good Lord, woman, what are ya supposed to be?"

"Oh, Roy, don't be so ineducated. Can't you tell I'm a sexy maid?"

"A maid? It's not liken you to clean anywhere. Why would you be a maid on a vacation in a real hotel? They pay people to do that for ya here."

"I thought it was sexy."

"The only time a maid is sexy is when she be bringin' me my beer. Now hurry up. I want to get to this big Halloween shindig before all the ribs is gone. They promised me ribs, and it's taken them this long to get them for me. I ain't goin' to lose out on them now. Move it along. We're supposed to meet Edwardo in the lobby."

Crystal flipped her hair back. "Is this the timeshare thing? If it is, I hope it is not an entire night of timeshare presentation. I didn't spend thirty dollars on a new outfit and get all dressed up to sit in a chair for four hours and then be escorted out as soon as they find out we don't have any credit."

"No, that's tomorrow morning. But who cares? As long as they gots beer and ribs, they can keep me hostage as long as they want."

The couple met the rest of the vacationers in the lobby. "Look, there's Bruce and Sally." Roy raised his arm and waved frantically, then whispered in Crystal's ear, "I'm gonna try to get Bruce here to play me in some cards. I bet I can win big from him. I don't think he is too edimacted."

Edwardo entered the lobby. "Good evening, I am so glad you are all here to help us celebrate The Day of the Dead." Edward rubbed his hands together and smiled. "Generally this holiday is celebrated in Mexico, but we have common ancestors and we celebrate it here too."

Roy brushed a greasy lock behind his ear, leaned over and snickered in Crystal's ear. "Me thinks Edwaaar-doooo has been celebrating already. He doesn't know he's in Mexico."

"Follow me please," Edwardo said as he led the vacationers to an open pavilion in a tucked-away section of the beach. Large hand-carved bamboo pillars held up a thatched roof. Edwardo turned toward the group. "We reserve this place for private parties for our special quests. Please, make yourselves at home while the staff and I bring the food."

Edwardo turned and walked back toward the main part of the resort, leaving the crowd unsupervised.

"Look at this, Bruce," Roy said, "there ain't nothing here but some long wooden tables and benches. I guess Edwardo was right. The only thing this is good for is private parties. I don't know why they didn't have the food and drink here already."

"I guess this is where they hold us hostage and try to get us to sign on the dotted line." Bruce scratched his behind. "Oh well, if a few hours of someone holding me hostage and tryin' to sell me a timeshare is all I have to do so I could get all I could eat and drink this week, it is worth it!"

Roy shook his head. "No, they said that timeshare

thing was tomorrow. Tonight is a Halloween party with more all we can eat and drink." He scratched his jaw. "And they promised me ribs tonight. I ain't doing nothing else until I gets me the ribs I was promised."

Bruce walked over to one of the massive pillars that held up the thatched roof and ran his hand along surface. "Good Lordie! Look at all these skulls carved into the pillars! What in tarnation is that for?"

Roy shook his head. "I don't know. Just some Mexican shit, I guess. I know I wouldn't want it beside my velvet tapestry of Elvis."

Edwardo entered the pavilion. "Attention, guests. Could I have your attention, please?"

Roy grabbed his crotch and shouted, "There's no food or beer here, so why not. Anyways, if'n you want attention, all I have to do is look at my wife's boobs." He drummed on Crystal's boobs with the palms of his hands, and his pride and joy sprang to life, jutting out from the costume's cheap pants. "See, this thing is at full attention now."

The other vacationers laughed while Edwardo cleared his throat. "Yes, sir, that is indeed very humorous. Now, if I could have your attention. As I said earlier, tonight is the great feast of the Day of the Dead. It is a sacred celebration for us. On October 31, we as a community celebrate our loved ones who have crossed over.

We have celebrated this holiday for 3,000 years before the time of Columbus. You will be sharing a great sacred feast. Enjoy."

With that he bowed out and let the revelry begin.

A dozen wait staff dressed in blinding white pants and T-shirts carried trays loaded with lobsters and shrimp, cheeses and sliced meats, and pastries, then placed them on tables at the side of the pavilion. Two waiters carried in a massive silver platter. On the platter, for all to see, were the ribs Roy had requested. The giant racks of ribs were glazed in a bright red barbeque sauce so thick it dripped off the edges of the platter, forming droplets and soaking into the sand, staining it a dark red.

Roy dived at the platter of ribs, grabbed a whole rack and tossed it onto his plate. He tore a rib off the rack and bit into it. "Man, I thought these were beef ribs they are so big, but they taste like pork." He shook his head. "Damn, that is some good eats. I don't know what they feed their pigs here, but they sure grow 'em big and tasty."

Crystal poked Roy in the side. "Maybe they have a nuclear power plant here like my cousin Cathy Moore."

Roy guffawed. "Well, I don't care if'n the pig is cross-eyed as long as it tastes this good."

The vacationers gorged themselves, and the staff

continued to bring more food and beverages as needed.

Edwardo again appeared and approached the head of the pavilion. "My dear revelers, as part of our custom, we will all partake in the eating of a sacred symbol, a skull carved from a single sugar cube." The wait staff began to move through the crowd with bowls of the delicacy.

Roy picked his out of the bowl. "Lookie here, someone took the time to carve a sugar cube into a skull." He shook his head and snickered. "Now, what in tarnation would anyone bother to do that fer?" He chucked his skull into the jungle. The sugar cube sailed through the trees and hit a large macaw on the rump. The macaw turned and screeched, snapping its beak at the man, then flew away.

Roy curled his hands into fists and shook them at the bird. "Come snap that beak over here if you are so bad ass. Yeah, that's it. Fly away, you scaredy cat."

The revelers continued to party. They ate, they drank, they disrobed and splashed in the water. They ate and they drank some more. Several hours passed and the night began to chill.

Crystal rubbed her arms over the goosebumps forming on her arms. "Roy, I'm getting cold. Can you go back and get me a sweater?"

"I got a better idea, woman." He turned to Bruce,

who had staggered by. "We are on a beach in Mexico; it's getting a little cold. It seems to me the only thing we are missing is a good bonfire."

Bruce stopped, scratched his chin, then patted Roy on the back. "That is a fine idea, but I don't feel much like gathering driftwood."

"That is the great part of my idea." Roy tapped his temple. "I do surprise myself sometimes with how smart I am. This pavilion here is nothing but grass to kindle the fire and big bamboo logs to keep it going. It ain't buried in nothing but sand, so we should be able to up-end it with some work. Hell, there are all these torches. We just push it over and throw a couple of torches on it!"

Crystal tip-toed over to Roy. "I don't know if'n we should be doing this, Roy."

"Ah, shut your pie hole, woman. This big hotel has insurance that will pay for it. Even if they don't, they got plenty of money. They can rebuild it."

"What if they call the law?"

"They ain't gonna call the law on us. We're Americans. Besides, I'm a ninja. Nobody can catch me!" He darted in and out of the pavilion, hiding behind the posts and jumping out again before coming to a stop next to Bruce.

"A bonfire it is then, Roy! Let's just push this down,

pile it all up and get a good fire going!"

Each of the two men placed a shoulder against the bamboo posts of the pavilion. "Together on three," Roy said. "One, two, three."

Moving together, the men put all of their force into their shoulders and dislodged the posts from the sand. The pavilion budged. "One more time," Roy said. "One, two, three."

The two men pushed again, and the pavilion gave way, collapsing into a pile of rubble.

Bruce grabbed a torch and shouted, "Come on, y'all, this fire ain't gonna build itself!"

The other revelers joined in, snatching the torches and throwing them onto the rubble. The fire blazed up.

"Now that's what I call a bonfire!" Roy said as he stomped his feet. He turned toward Crystal. "Come on, girl. Come give me some lovin.'"

Crystal jumped up and down, her breasts swinging. "That's my man! That's why I married ya, Roy. You know how to treat a woman!"

The crowd clapped and drank some more.

****

The party continued until the sun peaked over the horizon. Crystal, wanting to avoid the walk of shame, stumbled among the snoring bodies strewn in the sand and searched for Roy. She finally found him passed out on the beach. She shook him in an attempt to rouse him but finally gave up and staggered back to their room. She fell onto the bed and starting snoring as soon as her head touched down on the pillow.

Roy awoke to sand being kicked into his face. A waiter and Edwardo glared down at him.

"Mr. Roy, it is time for the timeshare presentation." Edwardo's over-solicitous tone did little to mask the look of contempt on his face.

"What?" Roy blocked the sun with his raised arm. He lifted up on his elbow and quickly rubbed his temple with his fingertips, trying to heal his throbbing head.

"The timeshare presentation, sir. It is day seven, and as you agreed, you must attend our timeshare presentation."

Roy brushed the sand out of his eyes. "Well, I'm guessin' there's no such thing as a free lunch. Lead on, boy. The sooner we get this over with, the sooner I'z can go back to drinkin'!"

Roy followed Edwardo to the lobby where the other guests had gathered.

"We will be going to the timeshare pavilion."

Roy grinned. "If it is the same pavilion we'z were at last night, you are shit out of luck, Edwardo, my man."

The rest of the vacationers laughed.

Edwardo smiled. "Fortunately for us, the timeshare

pavilion is another one altogether."

Bruce puffed out his chest. "Well, maybe we will have another bonfire then before we go."

Again the vacationers laughed.

Edwardo motioned the group to the double doors that led to the kitchen, then led the troops through the kitchen where the staff were preparing a large roast. "As you can see, our staff is hard at work preparing dinner for the next set of guests. Notice how fresh all of our meat is." They continued out the side exit of the kitchen and down a narrow path through the thick jungle.

"This one is sure out of the way. Can't we just do this back at the lobby?"

Edwardo smiled at Roy's remark. "Perhaps we could have used the same pavilion we were at last night, but that one is no longer available."

Bruce leaned toward Roy. "It's not like they would have taken us there anyway. They are takin' us out in the middle of nowhere so they can hold us hostage until we sign those papers."

The group finally reached the pavilion. It looked very much like the one on the beach from the night before—bamboo pillars carved with skulls and a thatched roof. Behind it, a cliff rose high above the trees, and a cascading waterfall splashed over the rocks below. A five-foot-tall throne was carved into the rock of the mountainside. It sat at the center of the cliff-side, drawing all attention to it. The knobs at the ends of the arms of the immense chair formed a human skull, and the headrest was carved into a skull and crossbones.

The waiters from the night before ushered the travelers into an orderly line.

"Boy, they sure like skulls around this place. They must be rockers like me!" Roy, still in his ninja costume, played air guitar. "Na-na-na. See, I may be getting old, but I'm still a rocker!"

Crystal smacked Roy's arm. "Now who's putting on airs? You've never played a real guitar in your life."

A huge scarlet macaw soared above. The creature circled above them several times, gliding up and down. It squawked and then dove at Roy, suddenly landing on the throne.

"God darn it, maybe the birds are bigger than this," Roy said as he grabbed his crotch.

"Is that the bird you hit with the sugar cube last night?" Crystal pointed.

"Hell, I don't know. All these damn birds look alike."

The macaw's feathers glistened in the sunlight. It stretched its wings, first the left and then the right. It craned its neck and stretched its back, arching like a cat. The black around the bird's face began to spread over its head and down its back. The red, yellow and blue of the creature's wings melted together, turning a golden tan. The tips of the wings became hands and then fingers, the wings slowly taking on the shape of a woman's arms. The beak slimmed down into a sharp, elongated nose, and the legs thickened and grew in length, becoming the woman's legs. When the transformation was complete, Carmen sat on the stone throne, her slender legs crossed.

Crystal rubbed her eyes. "I don't know what was in my drink!"

Roy's mouth dropped open. "Whatever it was, it was in my drink too!"

Carmen smiled, smugly. She knew what lay ahead for the people who destroyed her pagoda and indulged themselves to excess on her food, even if they did not. "Edwardo, please, bring me the first visitor."

Edwardo, accompanied by two waiters, walked up to Bruce who stood first in line. They grabbed him and tied his hands behind his back with some rough rope Edwardo pulled from his jacket.

Despite the large man's struggles, he was no match for the waiters. "What the hell is going on here? I know I said you would have to tie my hands behind my back before I would sign anything, but that was a joke." He looked at the waiters, his eyes wide. "You're awfully strong for such little guys. Let me go!"

The men did not listen to his command but forcefully escorted him up a flight of stone steps. "We are not at your service today, sir." They stood in front of Carmen.

Edwardo bowed deeply. "Quetzalcoatl, my goddess, here is your first sacrifice." Edwardo pushed Bruce onto his knees.

"What the hell. Let me go!" Bruce struggled to get back up, but the waiters were too strong.

Carmen smirked. "He's a chubby one, isn't he?"

Edwardo pulled a blade of obsidian, black and shiny, from his belt. In one quick strike, he lifted the blade over his head, catching the rays of the morning sun, then sliced diagonally across Bruce's abdomen. While Bruce made gurgling noises, Edwardo thrust the blade upward into the chest cavity and carved out the man's heart.

As he held the organ high over his head, blood spurted from the still-beating heart.

The crowd gasped and turned to flee. They screamed and wailed, pushing against each other, but waiters holding sharp machetes encircled them, preventing their escape.

Edwardo presented the heart to Quetzalcoatl. She grimaced. "Good Goddess, the man is so obese, fat is clinging to his heart. I can't eat all that trans-fat! Do you know what that amount of calories could do to my waistline? Find me a proper sacrifice!"

Edwardo studied the crowd and spotted Roy. He traipsed toward him.

Roy put his fists up as Edwardo neared. "If you're looking for trouble, you slimy Mexican, you found it!"

Edwardo gestured to the men with the machetes. "Look around you, sir. We have an army at our disposal."

Roy moved his head to the left and then to the right, seeing that he was indeed outnumbered and out-weaponed. He bolted to the side, but Edwardo grabbed his hands and yanked them behind his back, then tied them with the coarse rope.

With his blade at Roy's throat, Edwardo motioned toward two of the men holding machetes. "Get the woman."

The men shoved Roy and Crystal to the flight of stone stairs. Quetzalcoatl tapped her fingers on the arm of the throne and assessed the couple. "My, these are good specimens! Bring them up!"

Roy spread his feet apart and puffed up his chest. "You don't know who you're messin' with, lady! I know some powerful Mexicans in the States!"

Quetzalcoatl laughed, making her stomach shake. Then she brushed her hair back and composed her expression. "You mean the drug dealers you work with? Who do you think brought you to me?" She tossed her head. "We're Central Americans, you dolt! Mexico is north of here."

Crystal cleared her throat. "Ma'am, if'n it please you, I am no drug dealer. You can let me go."

Quetzalcoatl glared at the woman begging before her. "Please," she said, her voice thick with sarcasm, "you are no innocent. My men tell me you use enough meth to keep an army going for a month." She smiled, showing straight, white teeth. "Even if you were an innocent, you were stupid enough to marry this man. Anyone that moronic needs to be removed from the population before she can reproduce." She nodded at Edwardo. "These two will do nicely."

Edwardo raised the blade above his head once more, and in another quick motion sliced through Roy's chest. With his free hand, he pulled out Roy's pulsating heart and handed it to Quetzalcoatl.

After scarfing down the treat in one bite, she picked the meat from her teeth daintily, as if she had just munched on a cucumber sandwich instead of a human heart. She focused on Edwardo and smiled. "I am so glad we decided to go into the tourist industry, aren't you?"

Edwardo smiled back. "Should I take the rest of

them to the kitchen?"

"Of course, dear. We have another boatload arriving in ten minutes."

The Farm Stray

by

Rohn Federbush

Warning: This story's method of presentation creates an obstacle for the reader as there is no way to tell if this tale is just the result of the narrator's over-active imagination or is really, plausibly, what happened—which would anchor the story in reality in a different way.

In Michigan, barns on unfarmed lands are falling down faster than they can be photographed. A prime candidate, where a deserted house sags among close outbuildings, has an empty boat trailer eclipsing the yard. Furrowed fields dip away to the large barn a half-mile from the house. The homemaker's need to keep foul smells and worse flies as far as possible from the kitchen door determined the barn's banished isolation. She was probably a city gal. A line of sentry trees rims the last hill of cleared acreage, offering a cool place to rest for a tractor-driver's baking head.

The barn is set off to the east, behind a long row of buildings, leaving the wife's view unobstructed for a good two miles to the tree line. Someone loved that woman. She must have been a beauty to dominate the traditional farm layout of the county. Farmers like the chicken house within earshot. They'll tell you about the beauty of the first spring moanings of a cow about to calf.

The back door to the house is equipped with an odd drawstring latch that needed pulling in to lock the door. Back then, when the house was occupied, farmers saw no reason to lock their doors.

Within the fence, but still to the left of the house, a garden-implement shack sports a gabled window. Traces of flower-box braces along the wall hint that the wife would first see blooms if she turned from her pastoral view. The farmer's daily trek to the barn was evidenced by a well-worn path. The first building along the lane is a boarded-up outhouse.

She must have been one of the first wives to have indoor plumbing. Probably didn't even invite the busty grange ladies over to see it. If the farmer owned the courage to ask why she was so shy, she might have said, "That would be bragging."

He knew the Depression left her few alternatives. After her perfect, banker father shot himself, her options were to marry or starve. The farmer never forgot her silken trappings; delicate lace draped across his first attempt at a gazebo's love bench.

After they married, he was allowed to wash her bobbed hair. When it first outgrew the careful style, he offered to cut her hair with the sewing shears. She, no doubt, thought his attempt hopeless and hung her despondent head while he carefully snipped away. When he was done, her eyes were still closed. He took his shaving mirror off the bathroom wall, bringing it to her dressing table. He carefully positioned the mirror so she could see the back of her head, then asked her to look.

She jumped up with delight, threw her arms around his neck, and kissed him on the lips. "It's perfect! Where did you learn how to cut hair?"

"You let me touch the bristly pieces when we sat in your father's garden." His happiness kept her standing there.

She was so compliant, he undressed her. She shut her eyes on the bed. After their lovemaking, he knew he probably had ruined any closeness they might have known.

The farm suffered from his reluctance to leave her absent kitchen attempts. Maybe he even made her breakfast. Each step toward the barn must have cost him some expense of soul. A sturdy doghouse for a faithful animal was positioned to cheer his journey to the barn. He would smile boyishly at the shameless dog's devotion, something he lacked at home.

The next building on the farm lane was a corncrib turned into a woodbin. The shed was filled to the roofline. The decline of the house should have seen a similar lessening of the woodpile.

Several lesser buildings, a tractor shed and a machine shop ended the lane to the cathedral barn. The hay door dangled open, but it was sturdily held by stout pulleys and giant hinges. The well-made barn, standing as a rampart against the wind and rain, still held a safe tonnage of grain. A walkway led to the right of the barn where the farmer could stand to share his wife's view of the rolling hills, before he buckled down to work.

He was surely glad to tie up the unhappy watchdog each night. He wouldn't mind going in through the side cellar door to strip off his overalls and boots, before groping up the dark steps in his sweaty socks and long underwear, hoping for a smile but content with her smell or the chilly shape of her dear, lean shoulder. When particularly brazen, he might enjoy her quick slap after his lips touched the back of her neck.

"Not now," stretched into forever.

The vegetable garden to the left of the house was sheltered by the fancy implement shack on the south side and by a larger carriage shed toward the north road.

death.

My husband said it didn't make sense. I could stand my ground with the guy, grease him down like a Chicago hipster only to fall apart as soon as he was gone. I couldn't explain my reaction at the time.

When I got home, I searched my photo albums but never found the pictures of the house or barns I was sure I photographed previously. I kept thinking I'd find them. Finally, back at my writing desk, my mind slipped into the landscape of the abandoned garden and found the mayhem. I wondered what was inside the carriage house before the farmer wedged the combine against its door.

Engrossed in contemplation and sitting safely in front of my computer, the same spirit who had held my camera and shook in dreadful fear in the car, calmly let me see, with uncontestable knowledge, the days before and after a violent scene occurred in the carriage barn. The identical earth-bound soul used my eyes to recapture relevant photographs of her home. Whatever the source of my imagination, I found all three characters who peopled the farm.

****

1930

The farm stray was a Carney thrown by the 1929 Depression off an eastern campus to the road of minstrels with an elephant show. When he jumped down from the last wagon to pursue a glimpse of satin among the summer roses, she recognized his Harvard accent. She took in the wanderer, giving him a square meal.

The farmer enjoyed her educated voice released from the long seizure of silence, even if her glances were for the useless visitor, who threw them out of their own bedroom. She said she hated the stairs anyway, although the expensive bathroom was upstairs.

They moved their double bed down into the unused parlor. She asked the farmer to use the outhouse in the mornings to let the hired man rest his delicate lungs. And when she was with child, the farmer was jubilant even though she seemed distressed. He'd witnessed his animals getting skittish in that state too.

The added guy was more helpful around the farm, even suggested he should leave so the baby could have a nursery. Nevertheless, he stayed to carve an elephant's head for the cradle. The farmer helped attach curved feet to the crib.

Just as the farmer remembered to pay attention to his herd when spring births were in the offing, he began to check in on his wife's whereabouts in the house. Once, in stocking feet he surprised her upstairs as she was putting away her laundry. They hadn't moved her dresser down into the parlor. She was straightening up from smoothing her satin underthings in a bottom drawer.

When he startled her, she blushed and her hand went to her throat.

"You should take it easy, after you've been bending over," he said, going to her side. "Are you lightheaded?"

"No," she said as she sat down heavily on the hired-hand's narrow bed. "Yes, you surprised me."

He tried to take her hand, but she withdrew from him. So he soothed her with his voice. "You're shaking." His low tones worked with the cows. "Don't be frightened. You're not anywhere near your time."

She stood up and headed for the door. "I'm fine. Just don't creep up on me."

Eventually, the farmer found them in the jammed carriage barn. He was checking in again, to see if his wife was about to need help with the birth.

However, the cries he heard in the carriage house were from his perfect wife astride the nude body of his hired man. He didn't remember he held the pitchfork he'd brought along to husband his wife, until he saw it stuck straight up in the surprised throat of the Harvard stud.

Their girl child he planted in the garden, after he

wrenched it out of the defiled body of his unconscious wife. He nailed the bodies of the lovers up inside the empty corncrib. The farmer felt more crucified than they looked. A pool of blood formed under his wife.

He lovingly took a trip up to her dresser, planning to pack the birth canal with satin.

As he rifled through the bottom drawer, he came upon an iron ox-ring. It was too ugly for any bracelet she might imagine. As he turned it over in his rough hands, he knew the hired man had given the iron ring to her. She was hiding the ugly thing when he caught her kneeling among her fresh laundry.

He wasn't sorry then, for his anger or for his loss.

He put the iron ring and the baby's intended cradle out into the garden shed, before he stuffed satin underthings into her. He cut down several trees from the back lot, dragged them to the corncrib and stacked the fresh cut cords of wood to hide their decomposing bodies from view.

When he finally looked at them, propped up against opposite sides of the corn crib with only their heads visible above the precise stacks of wood he had chopped with his own hands, the farmer realized he would miss them. He took his comb out of his bib overalls and straightened his wife's bangs. Then he went to the young man, her lover, and parted his blond hair, combing it to one side.

At a breath or gasp, the farmer turned around.

His wife's wide eyes were open, but her jaw couldn't move because of the log holding her head erect. She whimpered and tears ran from both her blue eyes.

He had rarely seen her cry except in vexation.

The farmer put his ear close to his wife's whisper. "I loved his clean linen smell."

He busied himself with filling the shed to the roof, almost apologetically placing the last log in front of her face. Her frightened eyes recognized the end.

The dog shivered when he passed now, but never howled at the stench. The farmer began to sit on the front porch, a lot. When the dog died from neglect, the farmer buried its body just inside the line of trees on the back forty. Then he remembered bones could be identified. He spent a couple nights digging graves for the farm stray and his own wife. He moved the wood, buried their bones, and replaced the cords of wood. In exhaustion the first night before he slept, he felt he had done all he could.

The neighbor ladies thought his wife ran off with that young man. Through the long winter they courted him with warm dinners and knit scarves. They told him to forget her and saw his guilt as grief.

One of them, from the next farm, finally married the widower, but wondered why he dashed back to the old homestead, whenever he spotted anyone poking around with a camera—especially near the full woodshed.

Meet Alicia Dean

Author of "Scarred"

Award-winning, multi-published author Alicia Dean began writing stories as a child. At age 11, she wrote her first ever romance (featuring a hero who looked just like Elvis Presley, and who happened to share the name of Elvis' character in the movie, Tickle Me), and she still has the tattered, pencil-written copy.

Alicia is from Moore, Oklahoma and now lives in Edmond. She has three grown children and a huge network of supportive friends and family. She writes mostly contemporary suspense and paranormal, but has also written in other genres, including a few vintage historicals. She is a freelance editor in addition to being an editor for The Wild Rose Press.

Other than reading and writing, her passions are Elvis Presley, MLB, NFL (she usually works in a mention of one or all three into her stories) and watching her favorite televisions shows like Vampire Diaries, Justified, Sons of Anarchy, Haven, New Girl, The Mindy Project, and Dexter (even though it has sadly ended, she will forever be a fan). Some of her favorite authors are Michael Connelly, Dennis Lehane, Lee Child, Lisa Gardner, Sharon Sala, Jordan Dane, Ridley Pearson, Joseph Finder, and Jonathan Kellerman…to name a few.

Read more about Alicia's story and her love of all things ghoulish.

Q. "Scarred" is about a man who was injured (horrifically) in an auto accident a year earlier (and blamed for his fiancé's death) and the woman who has never forgotten her love for him. Where did you get the idea for the story?

A. I honestly can't say where the idea came from. I love the old classic movies like Dracula and The Wolfman, and I knew I wanted a Halloween-themed story, and the idea of a phantom-like masked man came to me. (I've never actually seen Phantom of the Opera, which, I know, is crazy, but I was told my hero was similar. If so, it was a complete accident :))

Q. We love the Gothic suspense tone of your story. Several years ago you wrote "Lady in the Mist" (w/a Winter Frost), another Gothic suspense, and many of your other titles fall into the suspense category. What authors have influenced your writing in this genre, if any?

A. I used to devour Victoria Holt novels. Those have really stuck with me over the years. I also adored Marilyn Harris, and her books had a huge influence on me. I love the dark, creepy, moody feel of them. In general, the writers who have influenced me in suspense are Stephen King, Dennis Lehane, Michael Connelly, Tess Gerritsen, Lisa Gardner, Ridley Pearson…I could go on and on.

Q. We are thrilled to include "Scarred" in our upcoming Halloween anthology. Do you celebrate Halloween in any special way, or do you lock your door and shut off the porch lights to keep the trick-or-treaters away?

A. Now that my kids are grown and I live alone, I don't do as much as I used to, but I don't turn my lights off. I love handing out candy and seeing the costumes. When the kids were little, I LOVED dressing them up and taking them trick-or-treating and to haunted houses. Sometimes, my kids and I will still get together and watch scary movies during the Halloween season. Of course, our favorites are the actual "Halloween" franchise. No better way to celebrate the holiday than with Michael Myers. <Smile>

Find Alicia here:

Website: http://aliciadean.com/

Blog: http://aliciadean.com/alicias-blog/

Facebook: https://www.facebook.com/profile.php?id=100008364070487

Twitter: https://twitter.com/Alicia_Dean_

Pinterest: http://www.pinterest.com/aliciamdean/

Goodreads: https://www.goodreads.com/author/show/468339.Alicia_Dean

Meet Elvy Howard

Author of "Grandma's Way"

When **Elvy Howard** was twelve or thirteen she was so flattered to be asked, she agreed to go fishing with her father so early one morning it was still dark. Hours later, after being warned more than once to keep her trap shut or she'd scare away the fish, sleepy, hungry and bored to death, she made a solemn vow to never marry a salesman, like her dad, who was never at home. And also, to avoid fisherman who weren't much fun, even when they were around.

Of course she ended up marrying a guy that was both and having two children along the way. Elvy also privately counsels clients with adult ADHD issues, and life coaches those facing unwelcome transitions. Still married after more than forty years, with grown kids and growing grandchildren, she is a devoted to her family and her writing.

Elvy's debut novel, "Love on a Half Shell," released in March 2013, tells the story of 30-something Rae Green who is given custody of sister's daughters late one stormy night. Rae loves her nieces, but instant motherhood isn't easy.

Parenting is a theme as well in "Grandma's Way." Read more in this Q&A with Elvy and our editor.

Q. The story is told from Caroline's point of view, and you do a great job of taking on the persona of a fifteen-year-old girl who has a giant "mad" on for her mother.

How hard was it to get into the character's head?

A. It wasn't hard at all! I was an adolescent female once, and have been accused (many times) of never actually growing up. I am lucky, also, to have a fifteen-year-old granddaughter who helps me stay current on teen culture.

Q. From Caroline's perspective, her mom is selfish and uncouth. She is the enemy who is preventing Caroline's happiness. From an adult perspective, a reader might wonder if she's exaggerating. Is she? Is the mom really that bad?

A. She is to Caroline, and after all, that's all that matters. The story's theme, how traits of selfishness and greed can be passed down through the generations, is what interested me, and even I was surprised at the outcome.

Q. Your descriptions of what Caroline pulls from the attic are very detailed. The items seem real. Did you pull any of that from your own experiences?

A. How did you guess? Yes, I come from a family of pack rats. I blame the Depression as the reason my grandmother, mother, and I were (are) unable to part with anything worth over a nickel. All the items in the story were from my grandmother's.

Q. Is there anything else you'd like us to know about your story?

A. I hope readers will note how each of the characters—Caroline, her momma and grandmother—

clearly see the selfishness in each other, but not in themselves, and how that lack of honesty extracts a price.

Q. What draws you to write about kids?

A. Having children was a life-changing experience for me. Becoming a mother motivated me to become a better person in ways I couldn't have anticipated. I wanted to share that kind of story in "Love on a Half Shell."

"Grandma's Way," being a short story, doesn't have that kind of scope. The character of Caroline is based on a girl I worked with in Juvenile Justice. She appeared normal in many ways, but had killed some elderly neighbors. She also had a very cold mother. I guess it's hard to forget some things, and maybe the way I work it out is to write it out?

Q. Similarly, both stories have strong mother-daughter elements—both the struggles and the joys. You've been a daughter, mother and grandmother. Which is your favorite role? Can you decide?

A. No contest! Nana!!! And here's why: When you have children, all you want to do is love them. But things like responsibility, chores, worry, and fears begin to take over, and you don't get to live that love the way you wanted to. With grandchildren all you have to do is love them! That's it! (And if you're me, make them all the delicious food they want.)

Meet Leah St. James

Author of "Blood Moon"

Leah is a worrier, a self-described neurotic who tends to imagine the worst-case scenario in response to brewing troubles. She hasn't decided if this leaning toward the dark side is what draws her to write edgy, gritty stories, or if the suspenseful mysteries and gothic romances that filled her childhood bookshelves somehow imprinted their shadows on her psyche. Despite (or maybe because of) this propensity for infusing her fiction with murder and mayhem, she still craves those happily-ever-after endings and the romance of everlasting love.

Married to her college sweetheart and the mother of two grown sons, Leah is a native of the Central Jersey Shore but now makes her home in the Tidewater area of Virginia. Her published works include *"Surrender to Sanctuary"* (2010, The Wild Rose Press; 2012 Edward Allen Publishing), novella *"Adrienne's Ghost"* (2012, Edward Allen Publishing), "Christmas Dance" (Edward Allen Publishing, 2013) and the award-winning short story *"Letter from Christine."*

Here, Leah answers questions about her new short story.

Q. Tell us about "Blood Moon."

A. It's a short story about a book reviewer who reads a true-crime novel about a serial killer 50 years in the past. The murders took place near where she lives, on

Halloween, and she lets her imagination run away with her.... Or maybe it's *not* her imagination.

Q. What made you use book reviewer as your heroine's occupation?

A. I have a friend who reviews Young Adult novels and it always sounded like a book lover's paradise to me (although I try not to think about what it's like having to write a not-so-great review).

Q. The moon plays a big role in the story. Why?

A. Yeah…I have a fascination with the moon and moon names. I've had the Full Blood Moon, which (according to the Farmers' Almanac) is another name for the Harvest Moon, in my head for a couple years. It seemed to tie in perfectly with a Halloween theme.

Q. Your heroine's husband is an FBI agent, which seems to be a common element in your stories. Is there a reason?

A. I guess I do seem fixated a bit on FBI agents. I worked for the Bureau years ago and always felt proud of that work. I wasn't an agent, of course. I worked for a group that wrote commendation letters, so I got to see the case files, after the fact, to customize the letters to the case. It humbled me to learn how much goes on, the hard work they do, that never comes to public light. So I think of FBI agents as good guys.

Meet Alexa Day

Author of "Three, After Midnight"

Born in Brooklyn and raised in the New South, Alexa Day discovered romance fiction during an especially dark time in her life, her first year of law school. Two romance novels tucked into a care package guided her into a world where strong, smart women discovered excitement and adventure with the men who claimed their hearts. Since then, Alexa's written erotica and erotic romance with heroines who are anything but innocent and enticing heroes who challenge them to make room in their lives for love. A former bartender, one-time newspaper reporter, and recovering attorney, she likes her romances with just a touch of the inappropriate, and her literary mission is to stimulate the intellect and libido of her readers. You can keep up with her on Facebook, watch TV with her via Twitter, and follow on Lady Smut, where she blogs every Sunday.

In this Q&A with our editor, Alexa shares the backstory for "Three, After Midnight" and how she celebrates her favorite holiday.

Q. Your story isn't quite macabre-ish, but it is mysterious…and just a tad freaky! The story is about a young widow (Deidre) who visits with her (dead) husband (Cam) each year on Halloween night, with some help from the living (Trip). How did you come up with this story?

A. Really, Deirdre's story is about what happens when you have to change your plans, something I personally hate doing. For the most part, I try to be a relatively easygoing person, but I find as I get older, I tend not to respond well to changes brought on by external circumstances! With Deirdre, I had a character who had really been thrown by changes, starting with the loss of the future she'd planned on having with Cam. I asked myself, "What would be the hottest way to make up for all these changes, at least temporarily?" This story is my best shot at an answer.

Q. I love the romance between Deidre and Cam. It's still so vibrant, so loving. Looking ahead, can you see a point where Deidre will be able to move on and find new love?

A. I've gotten this question before! The first time someone asked me this, I had to smile to myself...I think I left Deirdre with a pretty sweet deal!

Q. Deidre's Halloween costume plays a vital role in the story's background. (Cam has to run to the store to buy an accessory for her.) Do you have your costume for this year already planned, or are you more of a last-minute costumer?

A. I like to plan well in advance—I don't have Cam's patience! I don't want to pick through the leftovers after everyone else has gotten the good stuff! Fortunately, my place is filled with costume components, especially wigs, so I could throw something together at the last minute if I had to. But my favorite part of the holiday is choosing just the right outfit for just the right event, so I like to spend a lot of time tailoring my costume choices for the evening's plans. I haven't figured out what I'm going to do this Halloween, so I don't know if I need something for dancing or for walking or for being outdoors. If I had to choose right now, though, I'd probably go as Michonne from The Walking Dead. I've got a nice dreadlock wig, and I should be able to come by a little plastic katana with no trouble. Hmm. That's not a bad plan, actually. I'd get to meet a lot of sheriff's deputies.

Q. You write erotica and erotic romance. In your bio you say you discovered romance "during an especially dark time in (your) life, (your) first year of law school," and that you're a "recovering attorney." Have you ever been tempted to put that background to use and go the John Grisham route (attorney-themed stories), even within the context of your genre?

A. I used to say I would never in a million years write about the legal profession, but never is a mighty big word. Really, the law is a great place to put an erotic story. Lawyers have secrets they have to take to the grave. They live with constant professional pressures to compete with opponents and keep up with colleagues. Desperate people put their futures and their fortunes into lawyers' hands every day. And I've heard that some lawyers out there are rolling in money, although I certainly don't know any personally. Trust, secrecy, desperation, money, pressure—all those factors can come together in a pretty hot way. So maybe a lawyer story isn't totally out of the question. Maybe.

Q. Bar-tending is another of your past jobs. What's your favorite drink to mix, and why?

A. I'm a beer drinker, so my favorite bevvie is the michelada, which is a beer cocktail kind of like a Bloody Mary. You put a little lime juice and a bit of Worcestershire sauce (or a soy sauce packet, if your Worcestershire bottle is scary) in the bottom of a glass and pour the beer on top. Then you give it a couple of spanks of hot sauce, drop in the lime, and sprinkle on a little black pepper. Once, I tried it with a spoonful of salsa in the bottom of the glass, which was a lovely change. It's spicy and cool and a little weird, but they sure are refreshing on a hot day, and they really give lighter beers a more interesting taste!

Meet Renci Denham

Author of "The Timeshare Trip"

Renci Denham earned her bachelor's degree in psychology from St. Francis and her MAT in special education with an emotionally/behaviorally disturbed emphasis from Webster University. She is currently working on her Ph.D. in general psychology at Northcentral University.

Renci began writing when she became unable to work due to a rare arterial vascular tumor in her cranial bones. After a long battle and over 20 procedures later, Renci is now walking again and has regained her sight as well.

Renci took some time to answer a few questions about the story, and her life.

Q. On the surface, "The Timeshare Trip" is an irreverent, tongue-in-cheek examination of really bad/crude behavior. We meet Crystal and Roy, thirty-something newlyweds from somewhere in Missouri, who have won a timeshare cruise to Costa Rica. Quickly we discover that Crystal and Roy aren't exactly graduates of any school of social graces.

Where did these characters come from? Are they based on anyone in your acquaintance? (Don't worry, it'll be our secret. <grin>)

A. Well, to be truthful, my family tree does not branch off in all places. I mean, we do have a couple of branches but it is limited. On the other hand, EVERYONE knows someone like these people. It does not matter what demographics or "clique" an individual is associated with. The guy who believes he is the alpha male and is really just a complete idiot and uncouth is known to almost all. He may be the guy in the cubical next to you or your brother's third cousin…or even your college professor. But the guy who thinks he is "all that" and is really just an uncouth idiot exists everywhere.

Q. Looking below that surface, through your characterizations, you tackle bigotry and ignorance. Was that deliberate, or did that theme develop as the characters developed in your head and as you wrote? If deliberate, why?

A. VERY Deliberate. Why? (Because) someone has to.

Q. On their cruise, Crystal and Roy attend a special Halloween feast. She dresses up as a sexy maid (which prompts Roy to ask why anyone would think being a maid could be sexy), and Roy dresses as a ninja (which prompts Roy to act out his character). What is your all-time favorite Halloween costume (that you've worn) – whether as a child or adult? Would Roy approve?

A. As an adult, a Gothic vampire costume: a purple taffeta gown and Victorian boots, and the costume was completed with real fangs. Roy would approve of the cleavage and the fact that I got it on super-extra double clearance. However, he would complain it was too much crinkly fabric. He would probably say, "Good God, woman, I have less fabric on my tent, and that thing makes so much noise every boy mosquito within a 20-mile radius thinks you want to make the beast with two backs."

Q. Speaking of costumes, we know you have a strong affection for sexy high heels. Tell us about how that came to be, and about your collection. Do you have an "Imelda" shoe closet?

A. Well, I grew up in Appalachia. We used to wear bread bags over our one pair of shoes for boots in the winter. My first semester of college, a friend showed me my first Harpers Bazaar and Vogue…it was the '80s. Anyway, the pages were so thick and glossy and they smelled so good and there were these WONDERFUL pictures of fashion, and all of my new friends I met at college had REALLY nice shoes. So I fell MADLY in love with shoes.

Over the years I managed to amass an indulgent collection of shoes, but when I was in a wheelchair, I threw away all of my nice shoes because I never thought I would be able to wear them again. Once I got out of the wheelchair and learned to walk again, one of the first things I did was go shoe shopping. I still enjoy shoe shopping.

As to the Imelda closet, I do not have one closet specific for shoes. I do, however, have several closets with shoe racks where I have made several small shrines that allow me to pay homage to my foot wear.

Q. When you're not writing, what do you do for fun?

A. I'm a graduate student and a recluse who makes

J.D. Salinger look like a social butterfly. I don't really have fun. However, I do enjoy being with my friends and family. I like to entertain in small or large groups and I enjoy going to my friends' houses for social gatherings. I LOVE spending time with my grandchildren. We paint and bake and decorate cakes, read, and of course my granddaughter and I LOVE to shop. She JUST got her first pair of high-heel shoes…for when we play dress up, of course.

Meet Rohn Federbush

Author of "The Farm Stray"

Award-winning author Rohn Federbush retired as an administrator from the University of Michigan in 1999. She received a Masters of Arts in Creative Writing in 1995 from Eastern Michigan University. Frederick Busch of Colgate granted a 1997 summer stipend for her ghost-story collection. Rohn self-published seven novels. She has completed eight more novels, 120 short stories and 150+ poems.

Here, she answers questions about the genus of her story and her interest in its setting.

Q. You start your story by warning the reader that he or she won't be able to tell if the narrator is imaging the events to come, or remembering events that actually happened. Was that a purposeful choice when you planned the story, or did it just happen as you wrote?

A. The fictional story is, in truth, about how the story came into my head. Do I believe in ghosts? Well, someone was with me on that real farm who crafted the story (which is the question isn't it). Did I imagine the ghost to tell the story? I cannot answer that question because I, in truth, do not know.

Q. The story is set in a real farmhouse you discovered during your wanderings. Tell us how you became interested in old barns. What other interesting things have you discovered?

A. As I grow older, I feel time is neglecting my upkeep as the owners of the barns and abandoned homes neglect them. There will never be enough time to accomplish all I dream of doing.

Q. The wife in the story doesn't treat her husband, the farmer, with much (if any) affection. It's implied she married him out of desperation, but why did he marry her?

A. She was beautiful. He knew she needed to eat. She knew it too. Her crowd had abandoned her as fast as her father's leap to death had ended his financial failure.

Q. Is there anything else you'd like readers to know about your story?

A. My husband is proud to be a part of the story.

Q. In 1997, you were granted a summer stipend for a ghost-story collection. How did it come to be? How many stories did you write and where can we read them? Was there a central theme (aside from ghosts)?

A. Part of my Master's Thesis for Creative Writing pursued the theme of the Native-American's ghost dance, which says they will regain their original territory. I claim to be Shawnee because of my surname "North." When I see the casinos ruining lives with addictions to gambling, I wonder if the ghost dance did predict the demise of character in our land. Payback is not always attractive. I've written about 150 short stories. Red Wheelbarrow, Potpourri, Bear River Peace Anthology published one each. I often use short stories on my Wednesday blog. My website has links to the published work also.

Q. What is your favorite Halloween tradition?

A. Going door to door to meet the neighbors needs an excuse nowadays. That's a shame. I can remember when May Day included giving baskets of sweets and flowers to neighbors too.

Thank you for purchasing
Mysteries of the Macabre!

Also by Edward Allen Publishing, LLC

By Leah St. James

Adrienne's Ghost
Print ISBN - 978-0-985-3123-7-4
eBook ISBN - 978-0-985-3123-1-2

Christmas Dance
Print ISBN - 978-0-985-3123-9-8
eBook ISBN - 978-0-985-3123-4-3

Lights of Imani
Print ISBN - 978-0-985-3123-6-7

By Elvy Howard

Love on a Half Shell
Print ISBN - 978-0-985-3123-3-6
eBook ISBN - 978-0-985-3123-2-9

More information at:
edwardallenpublishing.com

CPSIA information can be obtained
at www.ICGtesting.com
Printed in the USA
FFOW03n1953250915
17230FF